"I want to make [...]
I will make amenas.

Cait continued, "You haven't asked why I came back, but if you'll let me stay until after our...that is, until after Christmas—the end of December—then, after that, if you want a divorce, or...or whatever, I'll abide by your wishes. I won't fight you, and I won't let my father hire any high-priced lawyers to fight you. I don't want anything from you."

"Do you want a divorce?" Justin asked coolly.

No, her whole body screamed. Out loud she said carefully, "My mother always accused me of not thinking of the consequences to others before I act. This time I want to do what's right." She didn't add that doing what was right for her meant winning Justin's love.

After a bit Justin said, "I have no objection to your staying until the end of the year."

"Thank you." She plunged ahead. "I know I have no right to ask another favor, but do you suppose we could, uh, try and be friends while I'm here?"

"Friends!" he said explosively. "You don't ask much, do you?"

Jeanne Allan loves travel, bird- and people-watching, reading, old movies, creative messes, red rooms, her two grown children, sometimes their pets, laughter and anything interesting. Having lived and traveled throughout the U.S. and Europe as a military wife, she and her husband of twenty-seven years now seek the perfect Colorado settings for her books. Jeanne, who was honored as Colorado Romance Writer for 1989, has always loved writing and telling stories and she hopes her romances leave readers smiling.

Books by Jeanne Allan

HARLEQUIN ROMANCE
3217—FROM THE HIGHEST MOUNTAIN
3286—THE COWBOY NEXT DOOR
3384—CHARLOTTE'S COWBOY
3408—MOVING IN WITH ADAM

A Mistletoe Marriage
Jeanne Allan

Harlequin Books

TORONTO • NEW YORK • LONDON
AMSTERDAM • PARIS • SYDNEY • HAMBURG
STOCKHOLM • ATHENS • TOKYO • MILAN
MADRID • WARSAW • BUDAPEST • AUCKLAND

To the man who keeps me smiling.
Happy Anniversary!
December 27

ISBN 0-373-03437-7

A MISTLETOE MARRIAGE

First North American Publication 1996.

CHAPTER ONE

CAITLIN VALENTINE stared in disbelief at the gray-haired man in the hospital bed. "Are you telling me, if I don't go back to the ranch and stay for a month, you're going to write your will leaving things in such a way that the ranch would end up equally divided between Lane and your precious Justin?"

Hank gave her a hard look from beneath sun-bleached eyebrows. "I thought he was your precious Justin. Gin."

"Again?" Cait laid her cards down on the metal bedside table. "It's not fair talking nonsense to distract me. I must owe you over one hundred thousand dollars already."

"Seems to me," the old man drawled, "you owe more than pretend money to Justin."

"How about what you owe him?" She concentrated on shuffling the playing cards. And on controlling her shaking fingers. "You've claimed often enough he's been your right-hand man since his folks died when he was ten. You know he does the work of three men on the place. He's earned the right to take over the ranch. I never heard you promised Lane's dad when he sold his third share to you that you'd give it back to Lane."

"All my brother, Wylie, cared about was getting the money. He didn't give a damn if any of the Rutherford ranch passed down to his son."

"Well, then." Cait kept her gaze on the cards she was dealing.

"If you feel so strongly about Lane getting back his share of the ranch, will him the one-third share Wylie

5

sold you. Give your original share to Justin, and that, along with the third he inherited from his mother, will give him two-thirds of the ranch and control.'' She carefully arranged her cards. ''It'd take more than a broken hip to kill you, so I don't know what this fixation with your will is about. I think you landed on your head when you fell, not your hip.''

''Me falling should tell you I'm getting old and feeble,'' Hank said in a plaintive voice.

''If you weren't so stubborn about getting bifocals, you'd have seen that board you tripped over. You must think I'm feebleminded if you think I'd believe for an instant you'd ever do anything not in Justin's best interests. Everyone knows he's your pride and joy.'' Cait picked up one card and discarded another.

Hank Rutherford studied the cards in his work-scarred hands. ''After Marie and the baby died, Justin was all I had left. I've always wanted the best for him.''

Cait gave a short, harsh laugh. ''And I was hardly the best, was I?'' Standing up, she walked over to the window and stared out. A gusting November wind attacked the few golden leaves remaining on a nearby tree. The sun had given up its feeble attempt to pierce the clouds hanging low over Colorado Springs, and Pikes Peak stood obscured behind a dark gray cloud bank. The snow that had fallen during the night had partially melted, providing dirty slush for speeding cars to throw at pedestrians entering the crosswalk in front of the hospital.

Watching as a woman yanked her carefree child out of harm's way, even from up here Cait could see the mud splattering the woman's legs as she scolded the child before giving him a fierce hug. Cait turned to face her husband's uncle as he lay in the hospital bed. ''You didn't want Justin to marry me, and admit it, you were thrilled when I left."

Instead of denying her words, Hank said, "Even as a kid, my brother, Wylie, had plenty of charm and not much else. But my sister, Mandy, Justin's mother, she was a pistol. Wasn't anything she wouldn't try and she didn't know the meaning of the word quit. I want her boy to be happy."

Cait barely managed to avoid flinching at Hank's words. She'd quit, running out on her husband on the first anniversary of their wedding. "Her boy is thirty-one years old." He'd been twenty-nine when Cait left. Six months had dragged past before she'd admitted Justin wasn't going to chase after her and haul her back to the ranch. She should have gone back then, but pride had proved an insurmountable obstacle. As the days went by, pride had been replaced by another emotion. Late at night, deep in her heart, a terrifying question haunted Cait. What if Justin didn't want her back? The question posed too much danger to ask Hank directly. "Justin must have laughed himself silly when he heard about your crazy threat." Walking back to the bedside, she absently picked up Hank's discard.

"He doesn't know, and I have no intention of telling him."

Cait sank onto the chair. "Why am I starting to get the feeling you aren't joking?" she asked slowly.

"Because I'm perfectly serious." Hank Rutherford looked squarely at her. "And I didn't say a month. I said until your wedding anniversary next month. December 27. Two days after Christmas."

Ruthlessly Cait stomped down an absurd hope that sprang full-blown from nowhere. "What's going on, Hank?"

"I don't know how much plainer I can make it. If you don't return to the ranch and stay until your anniversary, I'm leaving things so my two nephews, Justin and Lane, share equally in the ranch."

"I don't mean that part," Cait said dismissively. "Why do you want me to go back to the ranch?"

"Two years ago you walked away leaving Justin a married man without a wife."

Cait fiddled with her cards. "Does Justin want a divorce? Is that what this is about?"

"Justin honors his commitments."

"Unlike me. Go ahead, say it." She tossed a card on the table. "You always did think I was a worthless, selfish, spoiled brat, unfit to polish Justin's boots."

"Maybe I was wrong," Hank said mildly.

"You weren't and you know it, so what kind of game are you playing, Hank?"

"The game is yours, Cait. You dealt it." Hank ran his thumbnail back and forth over his cards. "I think it's time you played out the hand."

The clicking sound of Hank's thumbnail chafed on Cait's nerves. There was no escaping the truth—or the challenge—in Hank's words. She might be late coming to the realization, but she owed Justin for the problems she'd caused him. She had to do as Hank wanted. In exchange for ensuring Justin inherited what was rightfully his, she had to go back to the ranch until after Christmas. Until her anniversary. One month. Blood pounded in her ears. One month to win her husband's love. If she failed... No, she wouldn't think of that. "All right. I'll go." Cait slapped her cards down on the hospital table. "Gin."

Deep indigo clouds stalked across the night sky, blotting out the moon. The knobby top of a fence post detached itself to fly low over the road. An owl searching for prey. The headlights picked out the old ranch house as the car swept past, and one corner of Cait's mind wondered if Lane and Marilee knew she was coming back. Most of her attention centered on the large house directly ahead.

Everyone called the frame house, built in the 1930s in no particular style, the "New House". The first floor contained a dining room, huge kitchen and pantry, living room and what had been the parents' bedroom, later the ranch office and now a TV room. The second floor held the original four children's bedrooms and one bathroom. On one end of the house, a large one-story porch had been glassed in and converted to a sun-room in order to take advantage of the stunning view of the Sangre de Cristo mountain range to the west. On the other end of the house, a two-story addition housed the ranch office on the first floor and master bedroom and bath on the second.

Cait brought her car to a halt under a glaring yard light and drew a deep breath. Justin stood framed in the only window spilling forth light, a window in their bedroom. He didn't move. Not that she expected a welcoming brass band.

Leaning her head back against the seat, Cait tightly gripped the steering wheel with gloved hands. Almost three years had passed since she'd arrived in the Wet Mountain Valley at Justin's side. The Wet Mountains and the Sangre de Cristo range had surrounded the brand-new wife with bridal white. Cait had gloried in her love. And been triumphant in her victory. Justin was the prize and she'd won him. Only later had she realized the cost of victory.

With the engine off, the temperature in the car plunged downward. The cold would soon force her to go inside. Thoughts Cait had wrestled with all week resurfaced to wage battle. Hope warred with fear. One minute she told herself doing this for Justin would obligate him to stay married to her. The next minute she wondered if Justin would even let her stay. In two years she hadn't received so much as a postcard from him. The thought of looking Justin in the eye and trying to explain why she'd run away unnerved her, but more terrifying was the possibility that seeing her again might prompt Justin to seek a divorce.

For two years she'd postponed making any decision about her marriage, reluctant to disturb the uneasy status quo for fear she'd set into motion something that culminated in losing Justin forever. Not that she'd ever had him. That had been one of her silly delusions. Just as silly as believing Hank would carry out his threat. Hank loved Justin; he'd do anything for him. If she had a brain in her head, she'd turn the car around and drive straight back to Colorado Springs and tell Hank... Tell him she was a lily-livered, chickenhearted, pusillanimous coward? Cait touched the small horseshoe charm hanging around her neck and looked toward the ranch house. Justin waited at the window. What if Hank wasn't bluffing?

Unlocking the front door with her key, Cait let herself into the dark hallway. The lemon furniture polish Mrs. Courtney used, stale smoke from Hank's ever-present cigarettes and a hint of damp dog assailed her nostrils. "Nick?" No welcoming click of canine toenails answered her whisper. A small amount of light from outside trickled through the transom over the door and picked out the spindly hall coatrack. Justin's battered, wide-brimmed felt hat rode in its usual spot on top.

An unexpected sense of sadness settled over Cait. She doubted the house bore a single trace of her year of residence. She looked toward the staircase, feeling the cool charm at the base of her throat lightly brush her skin. Taking a deep breath, she headed upstairs toward the room she'd shared with Justin.

His back to her, Justin still stood in front of the uncurtained window. He spoke over his shoulder. "It's late. Trying to sneak in like a thief in the night?"

"I know I should have called to tell you I was coming."

"Hank told me."

"Oh. Well, good." Carefully she set her purse and bag on the floor.

Justin turned, propping a hip on the windowsill. "Why did you visit Hank in the hospital? There's never been any love lost between the two of you."

Because I wanted to hear about you, she inwardly cried. Out loud she said, "Curiosity, I suppose." Removing her coat, she meticulously laid it across the back of a chair. "When my mother told me about Hank's accident, I wondered if he would be as formidable when he was flat on his back." She laughed wryly. "He was, you know. One look from those piercing blue eyes of his and I was reduced to the level of a naughty child again."

"You kept going back to visit him."

Cait shrugged. "I felt sorry for the nurses. If he was hollering at me, he wasn't hollering at them."

"Hank said you gave as good as you got."

"I guess breaking his hip took some of the meanness out of him."

"You always refused to see that Hank's never had a mean bone in his body." He paused. "I admit he's not always the most patient person."

"He certainly has no patience for those who don't meet his standards. Like spoiled brats." Cait swallowed. "He must have found me especially trying."

"We all did."

Cait dug her fingernails into her palms at Justin's flat statement. His words were no revelation, but that failed to blunt the pain at hearing them spoken. "I guess the only surprise is that I lasted a year here."

"The surprise is you came back."

"Yes, well..." She'd planned to tell Justin of the pressure Hank had applied to force her back, sure when he heard, Justin would be grateful and let her stay.

Only now uncertainty and fear clogged her mind and stayed her words. What if Justin resented her interference? Justin had always been blind to the weak spots in Lane's character. Justin might feel his cousin deserved half the ranch.

Her husband was waiting for her answer. Clasping her hands in front of her, Cait twisted the gold band on her finger. Postponing the explanation would give her more time to decide exactly what she was going to say. "Can we talk about this in the morning? It's late, and I'm cold and tired, and I'd like to go to bed."

"I'd like to go to bed myself." Moving past her, Justin switched off the light and firmly closed the bedroom door. Shutting them both inside.

And then he was standing in front of her. Need and desire exploded through her body, and Cait swayed toward him. "Justin," she said helplessly.

"No." Justin covered her mouth with a work-roughened hand. "I don't want to hear. Not now. Now I just want..." His mouth replaced his hand.

His kiss was hard and demanding. His fingers dug into her scalp, locking her head into place. Preventing her escape. Not that she wanted to escape. With a tiny cry, she surrendered to his kiss, kneading the muscles of his upper arms with her hands before clutching him around his neck as if he were her sanctuary and her salvation. Her home.

With no pretense at anything other than haste, Justin stripped away first her clothes, then his own, before flinging the two of them down onto the bed in a tangle of arms and legs. Fiercely he reacquainted himself with her body, demanding, taking, immersing himself in her softness. Cait molded herself to him, hungrily meeting passion with passion. Later would come time for explanations and words of love. And forgiveness. Justin was right. Not now. Two years had been an eternity.

Justin lifted his weight from her. "Don't expect an apology," he said harshly. "It's been almost two years since you ran out. A woman, arriving at night, coming into my bedroom, smelling of perfume . . . I'm not made of iron."

Pain sliced through Cait as Justin's meaning hit her. She'd expected anger and recriminations. Undoubtedly recriminations. She deserved those. But this . . . She clenched her hands at her sides. "Are you saying sharing this bed as we did just now means nothing more than a man and a woman satisfying physical needs?"

"What else? Your marriage vows may have been a joke to you, but I honor my commitments. I haven't slept with anyone since you left."

Cait stiffened. "Neither have I," she said in a low, fierce voice. "I didn't go to another man."

"I'm well aware of that," Justin said coolly.

She turned her head in his direction. "How do you know?"

"If you wanted to go to another man, you'd have gotten yourself out of this marriage as expeditiously as you got yourself into it."

The cold, emotionless statement sent an icy chill down Cait's spine, and she shivered in the room's cool night air.

"Damn it, you want to get pneumonia?" Justin sat up and in one abrupt movement yanked the blankets from the bottom of the bed up over her trembling body. He slammed down on the mattress and turned onto his side, his rigid back an impenetrable barrier between them.

Clutching gratefully at the covers, Cait surreptitiously wiped the moisture from her face with the edge of the sheet before tucking the covers under her chin. "Thank you," she said, unsure if she was thanking him for the covers or for allowing her to stay.

"Thank you," Justin mocked. "Sleeping with you always was good." He'd deliberately misinterpreted her remark. "It's never until afterward I remember your body comes with a price."

Cait inwardly recoiled, but said nothing, and within minutes Justin's regular breathing told her he slept. His caustic words catapulted her thoughts back to that fateful December three years ago. For years her father, Rafe Montgomery, knowing work on Hank Rutherford's ranch eased up a little in December, had tried to persuade his old friend and Colorado fishing buddy to come to New York for a few days to take in some of the sights and sounds of the city. Three years ago, Hank had finally come. Bringing with him his nephew.

Cait had taken one look at Justin Valentine's tanned, rugged face, broad shoulders, lean hips and impossibly long legs, and she'd fallen head over heels in love with the tall, young rancher. Then his firm lips had curved in a slow smile, a smile reflected in smoky gray-green eyes, and she'd fallen in love all over again.

She'd been twenty-one years old and she'd known with total certainty she was going to marry Justin Valentine and live happily ever after. That Justin might have different plans never entered Cait's mind. She was Rafe

Montgomery's youngest daughter, and whatever Rafe's baby girl wanted, she got. And Caitlin Montgomery wanted Justin Valentine.

Cait turned her head and stared at Justin's wide shoulders. If she reached out her hand, she could touch his warm skin. Instead, she thought of those days in New York. She'd flirted and teased and thrown herself at Justin with single-minded dedication. For four days Justin had treated her like a younger sister. Amused and entertained by her, he'd held her at arm's length. On the fifth day she'd decided extreme measures were called for and set out to seduce him. Somewhat to her surprise, she'd successfully breached his defenses, and they'd ended up in her bed. Afterward, Justin had been silent for the longest time before coolly making her a formal proposal of marriage.

Cait's parents had opposed the marriage. Cait was too young. She hadn't been raised to live on a ranch. Hank Rutherford shrewdly guessed how Cait had manipulated Justin and furiously condemned her. Cait was no wife for Justin. Rafe and Hank raged, Cait's mother moaned and begged her daughter to be sensible, and Cait had stormed hysterically around the Montgomerys' swank New York apartment, crying buckets of tears. Only Justin had been unmoved by the raging battle. He intended to marry Cait.

Her tears had turned to smiles, and she'd sailed through the succeeding days in a delirious fog of happiness. If Justin's enthusiasm didn't match hers, Cait told herself he was the strong, silent type. Two days after Christmas, a week after Justin and Hank returned to the ranch, Cait flew out to Denver. Justin met her and they were married by a justice of the peace. Cait's parents and Hank refused to attend the wedding. Cait hadn't cared. Justin belonged to her.

Only he didn't. Three years later, that hadn't changed, nor had her need of him. After two agonizingly long and lonely years, Cait could hardly believe he slept within reach of her. Cautiously she slid across the mattress and stretched out beside Justin, barely touching him. Even in sleep, he was as yielding as a steel post, but the heat from his body wrapped around her. She'd taken the first step. She was back. The time was past for arguing whether she'd made the right decision or the wrong one.

Down the valley, a coyote threw his mournful song into the black night. Another joined in, then another. In a few hours the first streaks of dawn would pierce the sky. Tomorrow was December first. Twenty-five days until Christmas. Twenty-seven days until her third wedding anniversary. Twenty-seven days to convince Justin he needed her, wanted her, couldn't live without her. Twenty-seven days to prove she was the right wife for Justin.

If she couldn't... She squeezed her eyelids tightly shut, holding back the salty tears. There remained her ace in the hole. She'd returned and she'd secure Justin's ranch for him. Afterward, she'd tell Justin what she'd done. He'd have to let her stay. Outside, the coyotes howled again, a chorus of derisive yelps that echoed later in her dreams.

The wet tongue slurping in her ear woke Cait up. "Justin, stop it. I hate that."

"Don't tell me."

Justin's amused voice came from across the room. Cait rolled over onto her back, a maneuver that proved to be a big mistake as a large tongue bathed her nose. "Nick," she cried in delight. The black-and-white dog, part Border collie and part who knew what, barked sharply in delight. "You doofus dog," Cait crooned lovingly, "what are you doing waking me up at dawn?" Burying her face in the dog's coat, she breathed happily as the animal wiggled ecstatically, his tail frantically beating against the bed covers. "I missed you."

"Nice to know you missed someone."

Cait shot Justin a surreptitious look from beneath lowered lashes. He was zipping his jeans, his bare back to her. Hard work, not expensive health clubs, had produced those wide shoulders and rippling muscles. Cait's stomach dipped, and Nick made a small growl of protest as her fingers tightened reflexively in his coat. She patted the dog in apology. Unwilling to address Justin's comment, she said, "Hank insisted Nick would remember me, but I was afraid he wouldn't." Cait propped the pillows behind her head and pulled the sheet up to her chin. Nick stretched out on the bed beside her. "He didn't investigate last night when I came in."

"Nick's been staying with Harry. Court's out of town, and Harry doesn't like being alone at night. When she brought him over this morning, Nick must have smelled you. I'm surprised his scratching and whining at my bedroom door didn't wake you." Justin grabbed a clean work shirt from the closet and thrust his arms into the sleeves.

His bedroom. Cait concentrated on scratching Nick's stomach. "How is Mrs. Courtney?" she asked politely. There wasn't a soul on the ranch who didn't know Harriet Courtney, Hank's housekeeper, thought Justin had made only one mistake in his entire life. That mistake was labeled Caitlin Montgomery.

"Why can't you call her Harry like everyone else does?"

Nick raised his head to look at Justin. Cait had heard the irritation in Justin's voice, too. Gently she pulled on one of the dog's ears. "Mrs. Courtney and I have never been on a first-name, much less nickname, basis."

"Whose fault is that?" Justin asked dryly.

"She thinks I'm totally useless and have no business being on a ranch. She'd rather have spiders and rattlesnakes around than me."

"You're wrong." Justin picked up a boot and sat on the far edge of the bed.

She'd been wrong from the beginning. "I'm sorry. I never thought everything would be so wrong. You probably won't believe me, but I'm terribly, terribly sorry." Cait's vision blurred. "If I could go back three years and change things, I would."

Justin's hands froze, his boot held out in front of him. Without turning, he said, "What would you change?"

She wanted to cry she'd make him love her. Instead she said, "I'd change it so we never met. At least I'd change it so when I tried to seduce you, you'd laugh and walk away."

Justin yanked on his last boot and stood up. "You were only twenty-one. And so protected by your family, you were young for your years. I was older. I should have known better."

"No, it was my fault. I behaved like a spoiled child and ruined everything. If you hate me, I wouldn't blame you." Nick thrust his nose under her hand as if to comfort her.

"I don't hate you." Justin didn't look at her as he walked past the bed toward the door.

His calm denial wouldn't fool a newborn baby. Last night, while Justin slept, Cait had thought on what she had to do and the best way to do it. The first thing this morning, she'd promised herself. Now she could feel what little courage she had rapidly draining away. "Justin, wait a minute.

"I want, that is, I came because, well, I want to ask you something." He halted, his hand on the doorknob.

"First of all, I want you to know..." She clutched at the sheets. "Last night you said you found me very trying. I was too dumb to see it before, but you were very patient with me. I've been horribly unfair to you, and I want to make amends. I will make amends.

"You haven't asked why I came back, but—" seeing a slight tightening of his neck muscles and sensing his impatience, she talked faster "—if you'll let me—I know I don't have the right to ask any favors of you—but if you'll let me stay until after our, that is, until after Christmas, the end of December, then after that, if you want a divorce, or—or whatever, I'll abide by your wishes. I won't fight you, and I won't let my father hire any high-priced lawyers to fight you. I don't want anything from you."

"Do you want a divorce?" he asked coolly.

No, her whole body screamed. Out loud she said carefully, "My mother always accused me of not thinking of the consequences to others before I act. This time I want to do what's right." She didn't add that doing what was right for her meant winning Justin's love.

After a bit, Justin said, "I have no objection to your staying until the end of the year."

"Thank you." She plunged ahead. "I know I have no right to ask another favor, but do you suppose we could, uh, try to be friends while I'm here?"

"Friends!" he said explosively. "You don't ask much, do you?" His knuckles were white against the brass doorknob.

"I'm sorry. Never mind. I shouldn't have asked." She hoped Justin didn't hear the way her voice caught on the tears in her throat. Her crying had always infuriated him.

Justin swiveled slowly to face her. "I'm beginning to wonder if Martians landed on earth and switched bodies.

You look like Cait, smell like Cait and taste like Cait. But the Cait I know didn't have a humble bone in her body." His eyes narrowed. "What game are you playing at this time?"

"I'm not playing any game." Cait indignantly bolted upright in the bed. "If that isn't just like you, Justin Valentine. You are the most suspicious, doubting Thomas. People can change."

"Sure they can. But Caitlin Valentine from a haughty, arrogant, 'damn the torpedoes, full speed ahead', 'I'll do it my way' spitfire to Miss Humble Pie?" He snorted. "When pigs fly." Gray-green eyes filled with amusement. "Watching you pretend to be sweet and agreeable should prove downright entertaining. How long do you think you can keep up the pretense?"

She'd forgotten how sarcastic Justin could be. Tempted as she was to heave a shoe at him, Cait contented herself with fixing a brave little smile on her lips. "Does that mean we can be friends?"

"Hell, why not?" An answering smile curved his mouth.

"Thank you," Cait said primly.

"You're welcome." Justin's smile turned into a grin, and unholy laughter sparkled in his eyes. "As a friend, Cait, let me pass on my Aunt Marie's favorite warning. You dress like that and you're apt to catch your death of cold."

Following his gaze downward, Cait gasped. Intent on their conversation, she'd failed to notice the sheet had fallen to her lap. The chill bedroom air had hardened the tips of her breasts into rosy points. Cait yanked the sheet up to her chin. "Justin Valentine, you are pond scum. Of all the rude and crude . . ." She leaned over the side of the bed and grabbed her shoe.

Justin was too quick for her. He whipped into the hall, closing the bedroom door behind him. The shoe banged against the solid wood and fell harmlessly to the floor. Justin opened the door a slit and stuck his head through the opening. "Temper, temper, Cait. Your true self is showing. Not that I didn't appreciate the view of your bare bottom when you went after the shoe." He quickly shut the door.

Cait dived under the sheets. Justin's chuckles sounded clearly through the closed bedroom door. "I'm going to kill him," she said through clenched teeth. Nick opened one eye. "Don't look at me like that. I am." The dog closed his eye. Remembering something else she wanted to ask Justin, Cait jumped from the bed, jerking the sheet from beneath an indignant Nick. Wrapping the sheet around her, she rushed to the bedroom door and opened it. Justin was halfway down the stairs. "Justin, wait."

"Why? Find your other shoe?" He kept moving.

Cait hung over the railing that ran along the narrow upstairs hallway. "Is it okay if I ride after breakfast?" The way Justin came to a dead stop on the stairs gave Cait her answer. "Never mind," she said hastily. "I don't need to. I just thought..." Her eyes burned. Justin intended to exact his revenge after all.

"You don't need my permission to ride." Justin resumed his slow downward pace. "Meet me by the barn at ten." Reaching the base of the staircase, he disappeared around the corner. His voice floated back up to her. "That should give you plenty of time to move your things into the spare bedroom."

Justin's casual statement slammed into Cait with the speed and intensity of a runaway truck. He didn't want her in his bed.

Somehow her legs carried her back to the bedroom. Nick opened his eyes but didn't move from his cozy spot. "You're not allowed on the bed," Cait said, the words coming automatically as she headed for Justin's bathroom and shower. Then what she'd said hit her, and she stopped. "No, you're not allowed on the bed," Cait said slowly, staring at the reclining dog. "Everyone in this house told me you're a working dog, and I was constantly warned against treating you as a pet." Another example illustrating how her ways of thinking and behaving didn't belong on a ranch. Her spirits sank lower. Justin had not removed the dog because he was being polite. As one was polite to a guest.

The year she'd spent on the ranch, Cait had always felt like a visitor, an outsider. The only place she'd truly felt like Justin's wife was in their bedroom, where he'd been a gentle, controlled lover, treating her as if she were a fragile doll. Unlike last night when he'd fallen on her like a hungry wolf.

The thought came to her that Justin seemed different. She'd changed during the past two years. Justin would have changed, too. Or perhaps he was the same and what had changed was her ability to see Justin as he was instead of what she'd wanted him to be. For the first time, Cait wondered exactly what manner of man she'd married.

CHAPTER TWO

LEANING against the wooden corral, his scarred boots crossed at the ankle and his cowboy hat pulled low over dark brown hair, Justin epitomized Hollywood's favorite icon. All he needed were two six-guns in a belt slung around his lean hips. Nick trotted from Cait's side to greet Nighthawk, Justin's black gelding, who was saddled up and loosely tethered to a post. Someone had slung Cait's old saddle over the top rail of the corral.

Behind Justin, a half-dozen horses milled around in the corral, raising small clouds of dust. Feeling Justin's unswerving stare on her and remembering his comment about her bare bottom, a warm flush crawled up Cait's face. Avoiding his gaze, she climbed up on the bottom rail and craned her neck for a better view of the horses. Nick sprawled on the ground outside the corral. "Where's Rascal?" Cait asked.

"She's not here anymore."

Cait looked at him in disbelief. "You got rid of her?"

Justin turned to face the horses, propping his elbows on the top rail. "I'd hoped Hank had told you."

"Told me what? That you were so angry with me you sold my favorite horse? How could you sell one of your best mares?" Nick lifted his head as Cait's voice rose angrily. "Of all the mean, low-down, crummy... You never used to be spiteful." Cait clutched at the rail. "I know she wasn't my horse and you had every right to sell her and I did leave and I shouldn't have expected you to keep her just because I liked to ride her but you always said you were going to breed her and you know she'll produce quality foals so I can't believe—'' A gloved hand over her mouth cut off the furious flow of words.

Justin yanked her off the rail and pulled her back against his hard body. "I didn't sell her," he grated out. "She's just gone. Accept that, damn it, and choose another horse."

Cait bit down hard on the gloved fingers covering her mouth. Ignoring Justin's strangled oath, she turned her head and gave him a dirty look. "Which one would you have me choose? That ugly, yellow, swaybacked, knock-kneed, half-asleep slug?" Even in her anger, she was intensely aware of Justin's arm cradling her below her breasts.

"No. Look again."

"Hi, Cait." The voice hailed her from behind. "Hank said you were coming back. I'm surprised you're still driving that sporty little red number."

Justin released her as he acknowledged his cousin.

"Hello, Lane," Cait said coolly. Justin's cousin had been another who'd made it clear Cait didn't belong on the ranch. Cait had been forced to make it just as clear she had no intention of playing bedroom games with Lane behind Justin's back. Or behind the back of Lane's wife, Marilee. "I wouldn't sell my car. It was a gift from my parents when they couldn't attend my college graduation."

Lane posed nonchalantly against the corral, looking Cait up and down, his gaze lingering on her legs. "I suppose Justin told you about that bay mare you favored. It wasn't Marilee's fault. She never saw that patch of ice."

Cait felt the small, abrupt movement Justin made behind her, and, certain he intended to head off whatever Lane was about to say, she rushed into speech. "Justin was starting to tell me what happened. You probably know more about it than he does.'' At her words, Justin's hands descended heavily onto her shoulders.

Lane shrugged. ''Not much to tell. With that kind of broken leg, the bone splintered, and sticking out through the skin like it did, there was no way to save the mare. Justin put her down.''

Cait stared in horror at Justin's cousin. How dare Lane stand there talking about Rascal's death with the same detachment he'd use to discuss a beat-up old chair? The blood drained from her head and her legs turned to jelly. If Justin wasn't holding her upright with fingers that mercilessly squeezed her shoulders, she would have collapsed. ''She must have taken a terrible fall,'' she said faintly.

Lane misinterpreted Cait's remark as referring to his wife. ''Luckily, Marilee wasn't hurt, but Justin blew his top. You'd think Marilee deliberately caused the accident,'' he complained. ''It's not like he had to take care of the horse himself. He's the boss. He could have told one of the hands to do it.''

Cait wanted to lash out at Lane, but she held her tongue. Her anger would be wasted on him, and nothing could bring back Rascal.

Lane didn't notice her lack of response. ''After Justin got so snotty about Marilee riding the ranch horses, I bought her that little golden gelding.'' He pointed with pride at the palomino in the corral. ''His name is Doubloon, after the old Spanish gold coins. Isn't he a beauty? He sure puts that bay mare in the shade, doesn't he?''

''I've got something in my eye,'' Cait muttered, and, turning swiftly, she buried her face in Justin's chest, gripping the material of his jacket in her fists.

Justin draped his arms protectively around her as he gave his cousin concise instructions on some work that needed doing. Lane's boots scuffed the ground as he moved off.

"All right, Cait, let's have it," Justin said harshly, dropping his arms. "Get it out of your system and let's be done with it. Tell me I would have figured out a way to save any other horse, but since Rascal was your favorite, I murdered her."

"Justin, no!" Cait raised her tearstained face to stare at him in disbelief. How could he think she'd accuse him of something so heinous? "I know you had to do what you did." Destroying a horse was agonizingly painful for Justin, and it must have been even worse when the horse was Rascal. Not that Justin would have wasted a second lamenting unborn foals or unrealized breeding plans. His only concern would have been to spare the mare further suffering. Cait recalled Lane's words. Lane would have ordered one of the hands to take care of Rascal, but it wasn't Justin's way to duck responsibilities and pass tough chores on to someone else. "How could Hank even consider—?" She stopped abruptly.

"Consider what?"

Cait thought fast. "Telling me about Rascal. He was probably worried he'd have to deal with hysterical tears." Rascal dead. Waves of sorrow rolled over her. "She was such a sweetheart...always so willing. So honest. She had heart." Choking on the last word, Cait dissolved into tears.

Justin drew her close to his body. She wrapped her arms around his waist, comforted by his strength and familiar feel and smell. When she finally ran out of tears, he handed her a hankie. Cait blew her nose.

"I'm so sorry she's gone. It must have been awful, seeing her like that and knowing what you had to do." She dabbed at her nose again and squarely met Justin's gaze. "Honestly, Justin, I don't blame you for her death. I know how you felt about her."

"It's not much consolation, but the end was quick."

Cait nodded. "At least you were with her." She sniffled. "I don't feel much like riding today."

"You'll feel better if you ride." Justin wiped moisture from her cheek with a gloved finger. "Pick out a horse or I just might saddle up Double Looney for you."

"Double Looney?" Cait asked in spite of herself.

"What Court calls Marilee's horse. A dumber horse was never born."

Cait almost smiled. "Nobody ever accused Lane of having horse sense."

"He came to ranching late, but he'll learn. Now, take a good look and pick out your horse."

"I don't want to ride."

"Cait," he said softly, "you're riding if I have to toss you up in the saddle and tie you there."

Cait eyed Justin with uncertainty. They'd fought in the past, mostly over his ignoring her or putting the ranch before her needs and wants, but never before had Justin used that particular flinty voice to her. Cait decided she'd imagined the tone of quiet threat. Giving him a haughty look, she pivoted on her heel and started around the sleeping dog. Before she'd taken a second step, her feet were dangling in the air and a steel arm around her waist secured her to Justin's hipbone. "Justin Valentine, you put me down this very instant."

Justin deposited her on her feet facing the corral, penning her in with his long arms and hard body. "Pick a horse."

"I am not going to ride," Cait said with slow emphasis, turning her head to glare at him. At five feet eight inches tall, she had to look up to meet his eyes, gray-green eyes that had no business suddenly filling with mocking amusement. He was laughing at her. "I'm not," she insisted. Justin lifted an eyebrow. "All right." Cait abruptly capitulated. "Give me some room to look." The minute Justin dropped his arms and stepped away, Cait swung her arm toward his middle. Her fist connected with a wooden rail. "Ouch! You ducked!"

"C'mon, Cait, I wasn't born yesterday. Although I admit using me for a punching bag is a new technique for you. Where are the tears, the tantrums, the threats?"

"The only one making threats around here is you," she said with great dignity, cradling her arm in front of her. "Which won't do you any good, because now I can't go." Her voice rang with triumph. "I probably broke my arm."

"No, you didn't. You barely tapped the corral. Pick a horse."

"You have a real hearing problem today, don't you?" She turned away. Instantly, a large hand clamped around her bottom while a second hand grabbed her waist. Before Cait could protest, she found herself straddling the top rail of the corral.

Justin grinned arrogantly up at her. "One last chance. Pick out a horse or it's Double Looney for you."

In spite of herself, Cait turned toward the horses. "I'm not..." Just then she got a clear look at a little mahogany bay. The mare, true to her herd instinct, had managed to stay in the middle of the other horses, and Cait had barely noticed her before. Even with her shaggy winter coat, the mare was a dainty beauty. "Justin," Cait breathed, "where did she come from?"

"Who? Rosita?"

His innocent tone didn't fool her. All this macho nonsense had been directed toward Cait seeing the mare. "Rosita. Little Rose. I know I'd remember her if she'd been here before."

"Hank sold her as a young filly to a man over near Durango. Like Rascal, she's out of Rosalie and Scamp, and when we lost Rascal, I bought her back. She answers to Rosie now. I'll saddle her up for you."

Cait bit her bottom lip. "No." Every inch of her wanted to try out the mare. "Maybe later. Riding another horse right now would be disloyal to Rascal."

"I think doing what you love to do, riding a good horse under beautiful blue skies, celebrates Rascal's life better than brooding about her death."

An hour later, Cait reined in beside Justin as he leaned down to open the blue metal gate into the next pasture. It was still somewhat of a mystery to her how she came to be riding this horse. She'd been adamant she had no intention of riding today. In the past, Justin would have walked away in disgust, and she would have spent the day pouting because he didn't understand her. Not that she'd intended to pout today, but she hadn't intended to ride, either. Yet here she was. Meekly doing Justin's bidding, following him through the opened gate.

Refusing to meet his eyes, she looked everywhere but at him. From low in the southern sky, the winter sun beamed radiant heat into the valley, persuading Cait to unbutton her down jacket. Stalks of golden brown weeds threw elongated shadows on the large patches of crusted snow that decorated the ground. To the west, winds raised plumes of snow into the blue skies above the Sangre de Cristo range, while down on the valley floor occasional flurries carried the sounds of cattle.

Justin fastened the gate securely behind them. "When are you going to quit pouting and admit you're glad I made you come?"

"I'm not pouting and I'm not admitting anything. I'm surprised at you, bragging about your brute strength. If I'd have known what a bully you are, I'd... Never mind."

Justin walked Nighthawk beside the smaller mare. "You'd what? Never have married me? Never have come back? Never have invited me into your bed?"

Cait flashed him a dirty look. "Never have told you I wanted to ride."

"You didn't have to tell me. Crazy as you are about horses, I knew you'd be down at the corral first thing. You ride like you were born on a horse. I've always thought you were part horse yourself."

"Really?" The almost poetic thought intrigued her. Justin was hardly the poetic type. "What kind of horse?"

Justin reined Nighthawk to a halt. "You're as temperamental as a Thoroughbred, have the endurance of a quarter horse and can be as stubborn as a Shetland pony."

Cait wrinkled her nose. "Such flattery."

"I wasn't finished." Justin's gray-green eyes leisurely surveyed Cait from the top of her wide-brimmed hat to the tips of her riding boots. "In spite of that black, shaggy-pony haircut, you'd be an elegant, expensive horse with the spirit, small nose, wide jaw and long, slender legs of an Arabian." He gave her a lazy smile. "However, I don't think I've ever seen a horse with eyes of dark blue flecked with white."

Cait's heart skipped a beat. Asleep, her husband was an attractive male. Awake, focusing his attention solely on her, he was the sexiest man she'd ever known. Rosie danced skittishly, protesting Cait's sudden tight grip on the reins. Responding to Justin's look of inquiry, Cait said quickly, "I'm a little rusty."

Justin frowned. "When did you ride last?"

"Awhile ago." Cait nudged Rosie into moving. "It's been two years, I suppose."

"Are you telling me," Justin asked slowly, his horse keeping pace with hers, "you haven't been on the back of a horse since you left here? Why not?"

Cait shrugged. "You know how it is."

"No, I don't. I know you started taking riding lessons almost as soon as you could walk. Riding was the only part of ranch life you ever liked."

Cait looked at Justin in astonishment. "That's not true."

Justin made a disparaging sound. "According to you, the Wet Mountain Valley is a barren desert. There are no Broadway plays, no Metropolitan Museum of Art, no designer clothes, no taxicabs, no nightclubs, no Russian Tea Room and no countless other things any civilized person needs to live halfway decently."

Had she really made him think she cared about all of that? Echoes of her voice reciting the valley's failings rang in her ears. "Sometimes, when you made me angry," she said awkwardly, running her fingers through Rosie's mane, "I said things." Things to make him mad, to get under his skin, to make him care. Things yelled in vain to his back as he walked away.

"You were so young," Justin said, half to himself, "and spoiled rotten." Leaning on the saddle horn, he studied Cait through narrowed eyes. "I didn't know how to deal with you. I thought if I ignored your tantrums and headstrong behavior, you'd outgrow them. I'm not an advocate of corporal punishment, but maybe if your folks had paddled your bottom a few times when you were little, you wouldn't have turned out so strong-willed and demanding."

"Is that supposed to be some kind of threat?"

"If I lay my hands on that cute, round bottom of yours, it won't have anything to do with violence."

The provocative statement sent a warm flush of color to Cait's face. A split second later, the cold realization hit her that Justin had used the word "if". A magpie squawked from a fence post, and Cait stared fixedly at the large black-and-white bird as she fought off an urge to bawl. "Justin," she began, then fell silent. There was no way to adequately apologize. Expecting Justin to forgive her was too much to ask of any man.

Justin's thoughts apparently ran in the same direction. "Earlier you asked if you could stay until after Christmas. I said yes and I'm not changing my mind," he said. "Only this time, things are going to be different. This time I'm running the show."

"So much for our truce and agreeing to be friends. You already said I could stay and I know you won't go back on your word no matter what I say or do, so you needn't think you can turn into Attila the Hun or some tinpot dictator, because I won't have it." She urged Rosie into a trot.

Nighthawk thundered alongside and Justin reached over and grabbed Rosie's reins, bringing Cait's mount to a stop. "What you never understood," Justin said in a level voice, "is that I can be as stubborn and strong-willed as you are." Without letting go of Rosie's reins, Justin turned Nighthawk so the two horses stood nose-to-tail. Before Cait could utter a word of protest, he flipped her hat from her head and wrapped his free hand around her neck. "I think it's time you realized that."

He couldn't possibly be planning to kiss her, Cait thought, even as Justin's mouth descended. She grabbed the saddle horn with her right hand and clutched at Justin's open jacket with her left. His firm lips slanted over hers, demanding a response. Cait gave a tiny moan and parted her lips. Justin's fingers pressed into her scalp as he deepened the kiss. The discomfort produced by the awkward positioning of her body disappeared in the onslaught of scalding heat that poured over Cait.

Letting go of the saddle horn, she reached up to push away Justin's hat so she could weave her fingers through his thick, wavy hair. He laughed softly against her mouth and moved his hand from her neck to under her jacket. An electrifying jolt flashed through Cait's body at the feel of Justin's gloved hand curving possessively over her breast, and she eagerly pressed closer to him, sliding slightly sideways in her saddle. The horses moved restlessly, wedging Cait's leg against Justin's leg. His thigh burned through her old, threadbare jeans.

Justin lifted his head. "If anyone drove down the road and looked over here and saw us, they'd think we'd gone loco." He planted a firm kiss on her trembling lips and shoved her upright in her saddle. "Behave yourself."

"Me!" Cait gasped. "I wasn't the one acting like a total idiot, trying to kiss someone on a horse."

Justin leaned down from his horse and swept up both their hats from the ground. He beat hers against his thigh to remove the snow and dirt and handed it to her. Brushing his hat, he placed it securely on his head. "No," he drawled, "you were the one issuing a challenge with those pouty pink lips." He gave her a wicked grin.

Choosing to ignore the blatantly macho remark, Cait rode off.

Back at the corral, Justin swung down from the black gelding. He was at Rosie's side before Cait could dismount. One hand holding the saddle horn and the other resting on the back of her saddle, Justin looked up at Cait. "Ever since Hank called me and said you were coming back for a while, I've been puzzling over what you're after. I'm not going to ask you because I figure you wouldn't tell me. Obviously, whatever it is, it's important that you stick around here until after Christmas.

So I guess the real question is, how important is it to you?''

Cait studied the battered top of Justin's hat. She'd expected Justin to ask why she'd left the ranch and why she'd come back. She hadn't expected the particular question he'd asked. But Justin seldom reacted as she expected. He waited for an answer. "It's important enough," she finally said, adding politely, "May I get down now?"

Justin threw his hands up in the air and backed away a few inches. Cait swung her right leg over the back of the mare. Immediately, Justin snatched her around the waist and pulled her off the mare. Holding Cait against his hard body, he slowly lowered her, inch by tortuous inch until she was dizzy with desire. As soon as her feet touched the ground, Cait turned, spreading her palms against Justin's wide chest, and lifted lips imprinted with the memory of their recent kiss.

"Important enough," Justin coolly repeated. "What does that mean?" He moved his hands to her shoulders. "Important enough that you'll stay come hell or high water? Or important enough that you'll stay until the first time you're bored and no one is around to entertain you? Or somewhere in the middle?"

Cait blinked in the intense sunlight, curving her hands into fists as they rested against Justin's chest. "Come hell or high water, I'm staying."

"Are you?" The dangerous smile curving Justin's lips failed to reach the gray-green eyes watching her with cool detachment. "The last time you were here I treated you with kid gloves because you were just a baby from the city." He encircled her neck with his gloved hands. "I don't think I'll make that mistake this time." A suede thumb traced slow circles on her cheek. "This month could prove very interesting."

Cait carefully lowered her hands to her sides. There was no misinterpreting what Justin had said. He'd given his word she could stay. He wouldn't kick her out, but he obviously intended to make her time here as difficult as possible. After all she'd put him through, she couldn't blame him for wanting revenge. Not that she intended to let him drive her away. Or intimidate her.

No matter how he behaved, she'd grown up. Raising her chin, she looked him in the eye. "Thank you for allowing me to ride Rosie. She has lovely manners. I don't know how her owner could bear to sell her back to you." The amused knowing look on Justin's face told her he understood her strategy and was willing to bide his time.

"He'd overextended and wanted some quick cash," Justin explained, referring to the mare's previous owner. "You can ride her or any horse on the place any time you want." Justin dropped his hands and turned away, grabbing the reins of both horses.

Cait had one last question. "Justin, when did Rascal die?"

"A year ago March."

For a second, the daylight seemed to recede. "Three months after I left," she said shakily. "Why didn't you tell me?"

"You left us, Cait. I figured if you wanted to know how we were doing, it was up to you to find out."

"Why did you come back?"

Cait looked up from the camera lens she was cleaning. Lane's wife stood in the doorway. "Hello, Marilee." Cait recalled Hank's words from his hospital bed that Marilee came from squalor and poverty and she'd do anything to keep from going back. At his comment, Cait had felt guilty she'd never liked Marilee, but now, seeing her, Cait's old insecurities flooded back.

Lane's wife had been raised on ranches and she could cook and sew and bake bread and wash and iron and drive tractors and discuss pasture yield and calf birthing and when to mow the hay. In short, she was the perfect rancher's wife. Added to which, Marilee was petite and cute with a soft, curvy figure and rich, dark brown hair and incredible golden brown eyes.

"You're looking well," Cait added politely. As usual, next to the other woman, Cait felt gawky, and she knew her wide, fixed smile made her cheeks look like tennis balls. Her long legs, still covered by jeans and boots dusty from her morning ride, were flung over the arm of the large overstuffed chair. Cait couldn't prevent herself from running a hand through her chopped-off hair.

Marilee made a face. "Who cuts it? A lawn-mowing service?"

Not for a million dollars would Cait admit she'd cut it herself to save money. "Is there something I can do for you?"

The petite brunette widened her eyes. "I can't imagine what it would be. I mean, there isn't much you can do, is there, Cait? Except buy a husband with Daddy's money."

Cait could never decide which of her sins figured larger in Marilee's eyes—that Cait came from a wealthy family or that she'd snagged one of the most eligible bachelors in the valley. "You must admit I got value for my money," Cait said.

"Is that why you're back? To gouge all you can out of Justin in a divorce settlement? Forget it. The ranch belongs to Justin and Lane."

"That might come as a surprise to Hank," Cait said mildly.

"So that's your little game. When I heard you'd been visiting him in the hospital, I wondered."

"What did you wonder?" Justin walked into the room.

Marilee patted her immaculate hairdo and smiled with perfectly made-up lips. "If Cait would like to borrow Doubloon. He's such a wonderful horse. I'd ride him more often, but of course I don't have the free time she has. Not that I'm complaining. I'm old-fashioned." Marilee smoothed down her skirt. "I enjoy looking after my man."

"I'm sure Lane appreciates his luck," Justin said.

Cait crossed her booted feet and drew little circles in the air with her top foot. "I wouldn't think of borrowing your horse, Marilee. Thanks anyway, and don't let us keep you. We know how busy you are. What are you doing today?" she asked with spurious interest. "Grinding wheat, baking bread, canning pickles, or weaving cloth for Lane's work shirts?"

Marilee waved off the strangled sound Justin made. "You don't need to apologize for her, Justin. I know Cait only says those things because I make her feel inadequate."

"Can't fool you, can I?" Cait's foot waved faster in the air. Her fingers clamped onto the camera lens.

"You know, Cait," Marilee said earnestly, "I'd be happy to teach you how to cook. Really, if you'd just apply yourself, it's not at all difficult. A five-year-old could... Well, never mind. This afternoon I'm making the most darling Christmas tree ornaments from egg cartons and glitter. Which reminds me, Justin, Lane and I are going after our Christmas tree tomorrow. Since Hank's not here, we'll pick out one for you, too."

"No," Cait said even before she realized she was going to speak. "I'm getting the tree this year."

Skepticism coated Marilee's reply. "How?"

"The same way everyone else does. Chop one down."

Marilee rolled her eyes. "Have you ever used a chain saw?"

Cait wasn't even sure what a chain saw was. Managing to look straight at Marilee, she lied, "Our butler taught me to use one."

"Justin," Marilee appealed, "you know what a disaster Cait causes when she gets one of her wild ideas. I know where to find some gorgeous trees. Let me select one for you."

"If Cait wants to..." Justin shrugged.

Cait couldn't resist adding, "But thanks for offering, Marilee."

Marilee's eyes narrowed at Cait's honeyed tones, but she contented herself with smiling at the other woman's husband. "That's just like you, Justin. I know Hank gets disgusted the way you overindulge Cait, but I think it's sweet. If things don't turn out," she said delicately, "I can always find you a tree later."

Justin grinned. "Cait's tree can't be worse than Hank's."

Marilee shuddered. "The one good thing to come out of his broken hip. We won't have to endure one of those awful trees."

Cait slowly swung her legs to the floor and sat up. "If you're referring to the way Hank decorates a Christmas tree," she said stiffly, "I'm sorry you don't like the idea because that's exactly what we are doing again this year."

"Do you have to bait Marilee like that?" Justin walked back into the room after seeing his cousin's wife to the front door.

Cait giggled. "I thought she'd swallow her tongue."

"Don't you think it's rather childish to pick on her?"

"Me pick on her?" Mimicking Marilee's voice perfectly, Cait said, "I'll be happy to teach you how to cook, Cait. It's sweet the way you overindulge her, Justin."

"She can't help it if she turns pea green with envy every time you cross her path."

"I didn't choose to be born into my family."

Justin snorted. "Marilee's envy isn't about money. It's about legs that stretch forever, a bottom that nicely fills out a pair of jeans, a loose and sexy, devil-may-care way of riding a horse and an arrogant, aristocratic way of walking. It's about exotic looks, black hair, white skin and dark blue eyes. Next to you, Marilee must feel like the world's most ordinary, short, brown-haired, pleasantly plump woman."

"Well." Stunned by Justin's words, Cait wasn't certain how to respond. "You better be careful. I'll get a swelled head."

"You shouldn't." Her husband strolled across the room to her chair, placed his hands on the fat, stuffed arms and loomed over her, his tanned, angular face inches from hers. "I'm merely stating the truth. You look like a sexy, exciting, beautiful woman. You might even fool some into thinking you're a grown-up. But in this part of the country, outward appearance doesn't count for much. Hell, skunks are black and white and beautiful, even exciting, but who wants to live with one?" Straightening up, he walked out of the room.

The harsh question echoed painfully in Cait's ears. He couldn't have made clearer his low opinion of her. Justin agreed with Marilee that Cait was totally unsuited to be a rancher's wife. Clenching and unclenching her fists, Cait breathed deep gulps of air. She didn't need to put up with any of this. The stupid old ranch meant nothing to her. Let Lane have half of it. A phone call to her father and within hours she could be on the plane to New York. A battery of lawyers would ensure she never had to deal with Justin Valentine ever again.

Photographs on the mantel drew her eye. Slowly Cait rose and walked over to the fireplace. One photo was a wedding picture of Hank and Marie taken in 1960. Another pictured Hank with Wylie, Lane's father, and Amanda, Justin's mother, taken when Hank was a young man, Amanda a young girl and Wylie somewhere in between.

A third picture portrayed Justin as a baby with his parents. Cait reached for the portrait. Justin's parents visibly loved each other and were crazy about their baby. Cait had been born eleven years after her sister, Tracy, when Rafe and Keely Montgomery had thought their baby-raising days were safely past.

Cait traded the photo for another, this one taken when Justin was twelve. Again there were three people in the photo, Hank, Justin and a very pregnant Marie. After the death of Justin's parents in an automobile accident, Hank and Marie had taken Justin into their home, and, more importantly, into their hearts. Marie and her infant daughter had died in childbirth, but that sad event still lay several months in the future, and on this day, love and happiness surrounded the trio.

Cait had been drawn to Marie's face from the first time she'd seen the photograph. "I ought to hate you, Marie," Cait said softly. "You set impossible standards. From what I hear, even Marilee would be a distant second to you. And you know me. I'm not much of a cook, I don't know what to use to wash windows, I can't mend jeans..." She smiled slightly. "You'll be happy to know my friend, Sarah, taught me how to sew on buttons. And I did make a pumpkin pie last Thanksgiving, but I bought the crust, so that doesn't compare with your world-famous chocolate cake."

She touched her fingertips lightly to the glass. "I wish I'd known you, Marie. We would have been friends...well, maybe not. Maybe you would have thought me pretty worthless, too." Cait studied the woman's smiling eyes and loving mouth. "Or maybe you'd have thought anyone smart enough to fall in love with your adored Justin couldn't be all bad." Cait replaced the photograph on the mantel. "At age forty-five you were determined to have a baby. I'm determined to win Justin's love, so I'm not leaving. Besides—" Cait dusted the top of the silver frame with her finger "—I have to put up your Christmas tree. That's one thing even I should be able to do."

CHAPTER THREE

"I THOUGHT Border collies were supposed to be so smart. C'mon, Nick, even a dog who's only part Border collie ought to be able to point his nose at a chain saw." Cait frowned at some lengths of chain hanging on the wall. "Do you suppose that's part of it? Maybe we're supposed to fasten a chain to the tree and pull it down."

Racking her brain, trying to remember a movie or cartoon or anything where she'd seen someone using a chain saw, she studied the assortment of tools and implements housed in the shed. Her parents' fireplace in New York used gas logs. Hank and Justin burned logs in their fireplace, but she'd never seen them cut down the trees. All she'd ever seen them do was turn logs into small pieces of wood, and they'd used a chopper thing, an ax or something, for that.

"A dog born on Christmas Day ought to be able to figure out what to use to cut down a Christmas tree. Court said the chain saw was in here." The dog barked sharply. "Forget it. You're not my conscience. All I told him was I was supposed to get it. If Court chose to interpret that as meaning Justin wanted the saw, that's his business. Our business is figuring out how to cut down a—" Cait's gaze landed on a large saw hanging high on the opposite wall. "All right. The saw." She frowned. "I don't see any chain attached to it. And how am I going to carry that big thing on Rosie?"

She'd gone to college; she could figure this out. If only she'd majored in survival training instead of fine arts. Justin didn't have a whole lot of need for a wife

42

who could recognize the Hudson River school of land-scape painting or Picasso's Blue Period.

Hands on her hips, Cait slowly pivoted, once more inspecting the mysterious metal things hanging and lying about. "That must be it, Nick. We'll take some chain along and hope for the best."

Eventually Cait figured she was as prepared as she'd ever be. Nick sat on his haunches, his head cocked to one side as he watched her in puzzlement. She'd wrapped the large saw in multiple layers of newspaper to keep the blade from cutting anyone and tied a rope on it for a sling. Knowing Rosie would object to the bulky package banging against her legs or belly, Cait hoisted it over her shoulder and grabbed hold of a stirrup.

Rosie danced away, her eyes rolling at the strange shape on Cait's back. Speaking soothingly to the mare, Cait stood for a few minutes where Rosie could get a good look at the wrapped saw. "Okay, you know it's just me, so let's try again." The mare sidestepped the length of the reins and shook her head. The chain in a cloth feed bag hanging from the saddle horn clanked. Rosie pricked her ears nervously toward the strange sound. "Easy, girl," Cait said.

"What the hell are you doing?"

Cait practically jumped out of her boots. "Don't sneak up on me like that. I'm going for a ride. You said I could."

"You know very well I'm referring to that thing on your back."

"You mean this thing?"

"Yes," Justin said sarcastically, "that thing."

"Well, uh..." Her mind frantically churned. If she told Justin what she was doing, he'd insist on one of the hands going along to baby-sit her. She intended to prove she wasn't totally helpless. "Rosie and I, and Nick, are going for a ride."

"You already said that." Justin moved to the other side of the mare, rubbing Rosie's long head in passing. Leaning on the saddle, he directed a steady look at Cait. "But you haven't explained that thing." He nodded at the saw.

The mare nickered with pleasure as Justin absently kneaded her mane. Cait wanted to yell at the mare to knock it off, that Justin was her man, only he wasn't, except legally, so all she said was, "Well, uh, we're taking lunch."

"Let me guess. That's a baguette."

"Justin, quit asking. It's a surprise."

As Justin shifted his weight, his elbow knocked against the bag hanging heavily from the saddle horn. He gave her a strange look. "Court said you were looking for the chain saw."

"Did he?" Cait asked airily. "I can't imagine why he'd tell you that."

"He couldn't imagine why you'd want it, so that makes two of you without imagination. I, on the other hand, suffer from entirely too much imagination. All the way out here, I kept imagining you bleeding to death because you cut off some fingers. And I imagined you putting the gasoline in the wrong place and somehow managing to blow up yourself and half the ranch."

Cait hoped Justin hadn't seen her start of surprise. What did she need gasoline for? "As you see, I'm fine. And headed out for a ride. So, if that's all you wanted?"

"You're going after a Christmas tree, aren't you?" Without waiting for confirmation, he said, "We'll take the truck." Justin unhooked the bag of chains from the saddle horn and tossed it to Cait.

She staggered under the sudden, heavy impact. "I wanted to ride," she protested.

Justin led the mare toward the corral. "By the time Rosie hauled the tree back, you'd have nothing but a trunk and a few battered branches," he said over his shoulder. "Put that stuff away and meet me by the barn."

A short while later, a disgruntled Cait sat in the front seat of Justin's pickup truck. "I could have managed on my own."

"Umm," Justin said noncommittally. "I'm glad the chain saw was in Lane's truck. Not that you'd ever have convinced Rosie to let you on her back with it."

"Go ahead and say it before you choke on that hilarity you're swallowing. You know very well I didn't have the faintest idea what a chain saw looked like."

"That notion had occurred to me."

"I suppose the bag of chains gave it away."

"Actually, you gave it away when you said your butler taught you how to use one. I imagine Mr. McClary would be incensed at being called a butler, and furthermore, I doubt he knows much more about using a chain saw than you do." He paused. "Can I assume the chain was not for pulling the tree home?"

"Ha-ha. May I remind you I didn't make fun of you when you kept trying to get on the wrong subway in New York."

"Not much you didn't, but point taken. If I don't laugh, will you explain to me what you were planning?"

"Nothing very complicated," Cait said loftily. "I thought I'd chain the saw to the tree and that might make sawing easier."

Justin started coughing. When he could talk again, he said, "I know that silly sports car of yours would probably have gotten stuck, but why didn't you take one of the trucks?''

Instead of reminding him the trucks didn't belong to her, she pointed toward the forested hillside. ''I saw a tree I think will work up there the other day.'' When Justin pulled off the road and braked, she jumped out and opened the gate. Justin drove into the pasture, and Cait fastened the gate behind him. Cattle, seeing the familiar pickup, trotted toward them. ''You've already been fed, you greedy beggars,'' she muttered. Speeding back to the truck, she pushed Nick out of her seat and climbed inside, slamming the door and punching down the door lock.

''Some cowgirl you are,'' Justin teased. ''They don't bite.''

''Neither do turnips, but I don't like them, either.'' She wouldn't let him know his teasing comment cut deep.

Naturally, Cait couldn't find the tree she'd spotted earlier. For an hour she and Justin stomped through the trees in snow piled deceptively high, with Nick circling them. Jays squawked at the intruders from overhead, and a squirrel chattered a noisy warning.

For about the millionth time, Cait stopped to dig icy snow from inside her boots. ''I know I saw it here somewhere,'' she said, also for about the millionth time.

''We've passed up a number of suitable trees. That ponderosa pine back there looked darned good to me. Would you kindly explain exactly what it is we're looking for?'' Even Justin's boots crunching through the crusted snow sounded impatient.

''A Marie tree.''

''A Marie tree. What the hell is a Marie tree?''

''You know. One that needs a little extra love and attention.''

"Don't tell me you've fallen for Hank's mythical Christmas-tree story," Justin said in amused disbelief. "When you said you were going to do a tree like Hank's, I thought you were just giving Marilee a hard time."

"Mythical?" she asked in a hollow voice.

"The Christmas after Marie died, Hank hauled in the first tree he found. When I pointed out it was the sorriest-looking tree I'd ever seen, he immediately concocted that tale about Marie slogging through the snow, hunting for sad trees that wanted someone who'd love them in spite of their flaws."

"None of it's true?" Her spirits dipped to her boots.

"Marie refused to cut down a perfect tree—that part's true. The rest..." Justin shrugged. "Once Hank started the yarn, he couldn't admit he'd made the whole thing up, so he embroidered it year after year. Eventually the myth became reality, and he'd backed himself into a corner where he had no choice at Christmas but to put up a scrawny, misbegotten excuse for a tree. But there's no reason you should. How about this tree right here? One side's a little sparse, but we can stick it in a corner."

"Sure. Whatever." Cait slumped down on a fallen tree trunk. Rabbit tracks crisscrossed the snow near her feet. Nick meandered up, sniffed the tracks and rambled off, his nose to the ground. Cait didn't bother to stop him; the tracks were old.

Justin gave her a puzzled look. "Cait?" Setting down the chain saw, he walked over and tipped up her chin. "You look like someone stole your last dollar." His gaze sharpened. "I wasn't making fun of you for believing Hank's quixotic tale."

"I'm just resting." Pushing Justin's hand away, she hunched over, wrapping her arms around her bent knees. "Us city girls aren't used to hiking through the woods."

He dropped to sit beside her on the downed tree trunk. "Marie's been dead almost twenty years, and it's time Hank and I quit living in the past. We never bothered to ask you how your family celebrated Christmas or how you'd like to do things. I seem to remember there was a huge fancy tree in your folks' living room."

"Mother always had beautiful trees. She hired a decorator every year to create something totally unique." Viewed up close, the snow by Cait's feet was pockmarked and dirty. "Our tree was the envy of my friends. Their mothers embarrassed them by hanging up the ridiculous ornaments we made in school. My mother never did." Cait picked up a stick and poked holes in the snow. "The year I was ten, one of our neighbors gave me some pine branches she'd trimmed from her tree. So she wouldn't feel bad, I put them in a vase in my room and hung homemade ornaments on them."

Digging a pine cone from the snow, she kicked at it. "A few days later when I came home from school, there was a wonderful surprise in my room. Mother had replaced my stupid homemade tree with a gorgeous, small, pink-flocked tree decorated with dolls of the world. It matched my bedroom." Cait whacked at the dead tree with her stick. Chips of brittle branches rained to the ground. "After that, I was really too old to have a tree in my bedroom," she added in a monotone.

Justin packed a clump of snow into a ball and hurled it at a juniper tree. "Forget your mother's trees and Hank's trumped-up legend. You can have any kind of Christmas tree you want."

Cait took a deep breath. The smell of wood smoke from houses in the valley hung in the air. Pretending he'd known all along the rabbit tracks were old, Nick wandered back and laid his nose on Cait's knee. She absently scratched behind the dog's ears. "Hank will be home by Christmas, and I think it would be nice to continue the tradition for him. Don't you see, Justin?'' she asked in a low voice, not looking at him. ''Marie's tree isn't a myth. It's a symbol. A symbol of how much Hank loved Marie.''

Justin burst into laughter. ''I'm sorry, Cait,'' he choked out, ''but the only thing those trees symbolize is Hank's stubbornness. Rather than admit twenty years ago he'd selected the world's ugliest tree, he made up this fairy tale that he'll take to the grave, insisting it's the absolute truth.''

Furious, Cait jumped up from her perch. ''I don't know why I bothered to say anything to you. You couldn't possibly understand—'' she gave Justin a big shove, toppling him over backward into a crusted drift of snow ''—because you don't know the first thing about love.'' She spun around to march back to the pickup truck. A solid arm snaked around her thighs and yanked her off her feet. She landed solidly on top of Justin.

''Damn, you're no lightweight.'' Sheepskin-clad steel arms imprisoned Cait's flailing body, while eyes the color of grayed jade laughed up at her.

''And you're no gentleman, calling me fat!'' She tried to roll off him, but he held her fast.

''Fat?'' Justin's hands trailed up her legs to settle on her bottom. ''You're definitely not fat.''

Heat that had nothing to do with sunshine or winter clothing melted Cait's urge to move. Justin's hat had tumbled off when he fell and a small breeze played with the waves in his dark brown hair. If she reached up with her hand, she could trace his strong jawline and angular face. His high, jutting cheekbones made her wonder if a long-ago ancestor had mated with a Native American maiden. Hours of outdoor work had tanned his skin and etched squint lines from the corners of his eyes. Justin's heavy eyebrows arched in inquiry. Crossing her fore-arms on his chest, Cait eyed him severely. "What are you doing lying down on the job when you're supposed to be chopping down a tree?"

"Did I ever tell you you have a cute little nose?"

"It's too little," she said instantly. "It makes my mouth look a million miles wide."

"I like your mouth. When it's smiling. Or doing this." Tossing aside her hat, he pulled her head down to his.

The cold air had chilled his lips, but the inside of his mouth and his tongue warmed Cait to the tips of her booted feet. Without removing her lips from his, she discarded her gloves and lightly caressed his wind-roughened face with her fingertips. Justin's hands slid beneath her heavy jacket and moved slowly up her back. He'd removed his gloves, and his fingers heated her skin through her flannel shirt. Bringing his hands to her sides, he hesitated before reaching his thumbs around to find the sensitive tips of her breasts.

Cait wrapped her hands around Justin's head, barely noticing the cold snow beneath him. At that moment, her entire world consisted of her husband's kisses. Then Justin lurched as something solid rammed between them. Breaking off the kiss, he started laughing again. Cait followed his gaze. Nick was trying to burrow his way between them.

"Get your own girl," Justin playfully snarled at the dog. Nick bent his forelegs to the ground and barked sharply in Justin's face. Reaching out, Justin tussled the dog to the ground. "Are you jealous, old man, because you're too old to be carousing around with young women?"

Nick had ruined the mood and the moment. Avoiding Justin's gaze, Cait got to her feet and picked up her hat.

Spying her gloves, she retrieved them, shaking off the snow.

"Lady, people bring back a lot of things from the big city, but you're the first I've heard of who's brought back a fondness for kissing outdoors."

Justin had no business giving her a slow, sexy, stomach-dipping smile like that. "You started it."

Justin collected his scattered gloves and hat and the chain saw. "Are you saying you weren't willing to finish it?"

"I've never been a fan of that kind of outdoor activity," she said stiffly.

"I seem to recall a certain February night, coming home late from a party. There was a full moon, new-fallen snow and a horse blanket thrown on the ground inside a clump of trees. I had to carry you back to the truck because you lost one of your party shoes. Didn't find it until the next day. At least, that's what I remember. What do you remember?"

Her face felt bright crimson. "I remember we're supposed to be cutting down a Christmas tree." She looked wildly around her. Then took a second look. "There it is—" she charged clumsily through the snow "—the tree I saw before."

Justin started up the chain saw, and in no time the scrawny, misshapen pine was stowed in the pickup bed. They headed back down through the pasture to the road.

Cait shivered, waiting for the heater to warm the pickup. The sun hung low in the southwest, and chilly, dark shadows crept east from the Sangre de Cristos across the valley floor. A large hawk, intent on dinner, took wing from his perch atop a telephone pole and swooped low. Cait looked away. To the north, a windmill was silhouetted against a low, rose-tinged cloud bank. Hues of pink and peach colored the eastern sky.

A familiar shape caught Cait's eye. "Justin, look. Pikes Peak." The fourteen thousand plus mountain towering over Colorado Springs had kept her in that Front Range city when she'd run from the ranch. Visible from a long distance out on the Great Plains, the peak had been a beacon for weary pioneer travelers from the East. For two years it had also been a beacon for Cait's lonely heart. Each day, looking up at the peak, she took comfort in the knowledge that she and Justin, while apart in so many ways, at least were able to see the same mountaintop, even if from different sides.

The setting sun cast a rosy glow on the tip of the peak. "It's so beautiful," Cait said softly. "Do you remember when I first moved here, how awed I was by the mountains? I couldn't believe they weren't closer than they are. They seem so near. You told me how people moving west in the 1800s looked across Kansas day after day sure they would reach the base of Pikes Peak that night. 'Pikes Peak or Bust'. It beckoned them like the promised land."

"I don't remember," Justin said curtly. "I imagine I told you all sorts of things."

He'd never told her he loved her.

Justin sat in the office scowling at the sheaf of papers in his hand. Reluctant to disturb him, Cait hovered in the doorway, her gaze greedily devouring every square inch of him from his mussed dark brown hair to the well-worn boots propped on the battered old desk.

He must have felt her eyes on him because without looking up he said, "If you were a secretary, I'd hire you on the spot. Top dollar, no questions asked."

Cait moved into the room and perched on the dining room chair that served for visitors. "That bad?" Her year's stay had taught her that paperwork was the bane of most ranchers' lives.

Justin ran impatient fingers through his hair, which explained its disheveled state. "Hank insisted on doing the paperwork, and he never welcomed input from me. He's successfully run this ranch since his dad died, and bills were always paid on time and supplies ordered. Lately, he'd slowed down some and spent less time outdoors, which meant I had to spend more time dealing with the outside stuff.

"Hell, I didn't mind, but I should have paid more attention to this inside stuff." His fingers moved destructively through his hair again. "We bought a new computer, and he promised he'd use it, but he hasn't. I hate to keep bothering him in the nursing home, but I could spend half my life figuring out..." He waved his hand absently at Cait, his attention still on the papers. "Oh, well, it's not your problem."

Cait set her camera on the tall filing cabinet. "I'm not a secretary and I'm sure not worth top dollar, but I'd be happy to help, if you'll tell me what to do. That is," she said diffidently, "if you want help from me."

"Want it? Hell, I'd let Nick help if he'd offer." Leaping from the office chair, Justin quickly peeled Cait's jacket off her and installed her in the chair he'd vacated. "Hank put notes on things he'd done something about, so start with sorting stuff. Bills in two piles, paid and unpaid. Calving records in another pile. Correspondence in another. You get the idea. Sort however it makes sense to you. I'll get back to you." He exited through the outside door before Cait could ask any questions.

Her stomach sank as she viewed the foot-high pile on the desk. Riding Rosie this morning had seemed like a good idea earlier; now it seemed like heaven on earth.

With a sigh, Cait picked up the handful of papers Justin had abandoned in his haste to escape.

Two hours later she leaned back, stretched weary shoulder muscles and looked at the piles of papers decorating every surface in the office. No wonder Justin had been about to rip out his hair. "If Hank filed or threw away a single piece of paper in the past six months, I'd be surprised," she said to Nick, who was dozing on the floor in a patch of sunlight.

Hank wasn't the only one spending more time indoors. Although Nick occasionally accompanied Rosie and Cait on their daily rides, he suffered from bouts of arthritis and some days refused to venture far from hearth and home. Two of his sons had taken over his cattle-herding duties.

Cait stared out the window at the gray clouds building up to the southwest. The cloud bank obscured some of the peaks of the Sangre de Cristos. A gust of wind riffled a brown clump of vegetation outside the office window and a small gray bird took flight. In a distant pasture, cattle were lined up eating the hay that had been dumped earlier. Scattered through the pastures, baled hay formed huge tarp-covered mounds. Nearer the ranch, the immense bulls, with their massive necks and ringed noses, moved majestically around a pasture reserved for their exclusive use.

Movement caught Cait's eye and she looked down the road to see Marilee hanging a Christmas wreath on the door of the original ranch house. Built around the turn of the century and abandoned when the New House was built, the log home had been later renovated for a married couple who worked on the ranch before the Courtneys came. The Courtneys preferred the small, nondescript house built in the sixties across the road from the log house, Harriet Courtney saying the old home with its nooks and crannies attracted too much dust.

No mote of dust would dare challenge Marilee's housekeeping skills. Lane removed his shoes before he entered the house. And probably his clothes, Cait thought, thinking of the numerous doilies and knick-knacks that filled their house. "Too filled and too cute," Cait said to Nick. Cait's mother would break out in hives if she saw it.

Cait's mother would break out in hives if she saw this house. Not that Cait hadn't had ideas about redecorating. No one could live in a home constantly being redone by the best and most expensive decorators and designers on the East Coast and not have learned a thing or two. Except those decorators and designers had never passed on the secret for dealing with a house where two men had lived alone for almost twenty years in perfect comfort.

Once, to bait Justin and Hank, Cait had suggested painting the living room walls black and buying white upholstered furniture. Hank had bellowed like a sick cow. Justin had laughed. Lane and Marilee had been at dinner that night, and Marilee had earnestly explained to Cait why white furniture wouldn't be a good idea on a ranch. Cait stifled a small sigh and pushed her chair back to the desk. Marilee was hard to like.

Cait picked up a letter. Pulling it far enough out of the envelope to determine it was a business letter, she tossed it toward the appropriate pile. The letter was sailing through the air before what she'd seen registered on her. Her name. Slowly Cait stood up and walked over to where she'd tossed the letter. One word of the return address on the envelope leaped up at her. Investigations. She stared down at the envelope addressed to Hank. The letter was none of her business. Just because the return address sounded like a private detective agency, and just because the agency was located in Colorado Springs and just because she'd imagined she'd seen her name on the letter inside... The letter was private.

Reaching down, Cait picked it up. The folded paper slid easily from the envelope. A penciled notation in Hank's handwriting caught her eye. In big block letters he'd written the word "money" followed by three question marks. Cait stumbled to the office chair and sat down to read the letter.

A few minutes later she shook her head in dazed disbelief. Justin had hired a private detective to follow her. For two years she'd been spied on, her every movement, her every friend reported on. No wonder Justin had been so sure she'd not been with another man. He probably knew how many times she'd brushed her teeth and what she ate each morning for breakfast. She'd already read the letter three times. She read it again.

The letter was dated a few days before Hank broke his hip. It was obviously the latest in a series of monthly reports. Would next month's letter report she'd visited Hank in the hospital? Would the reports, the spying, stop now that she'd returned to the ranch? Two unmarried hands lived in a house trailer parked on concrete blocks near the Courtneys' house. Cait knew Joe from before, but Terry was new. Maybe Terry was another detective, hired to spy on her here at the ranch. The signature on the letter read W. E. Trace, but maybe Terry wasn't Terry's real name. And maybe W. E. Trace wasn't W. E. Trace's real name, either. W. E. Trace was a little too appropriate for a private detective to be true.

What difference did it make? The issue wasn't Terry or W. E. Trace. The issue was that Justin had paid a loathsome, dirty little creep to spy on her. To watch her, to peek in her windows, to go through her trash, tap her phone. She closed her eyes, trembling with waves of anger and pain. Had he invaded her apartment? Gone through her drawers?

She was too angry for tears. Her hands shook so badly she could barely hold the letter to read it again. The detective reported her activities had been the usual—work, class, tutoring, dinner with Sarah and family. She'd shopped for groceries, and Sarah's husband had changed the oil in her car. She hadn't gone to—he named a bank. Cait frowned. Why would she? She banked elsewhere.

The letter told her everything. And nothing. Hank's notation at the bottom of the page confused her. What did it mean? There had to be more letters. Feverishly she pawed through the remaining papers on the desk, but she found no other letters from the detective agency. A quick check of the mail she'd already sorted failed to turn up another letter.

The filing cabinet across the room drew her eye. Miraculously her legs carried her across the floor. There were four drawers crammed with files. Cait started at the top. The letters were in the back of the bottom drawer in a yellow file. She hated yellow.

She read every one of the letters. Reports more than letters. If W. E. Trace had peeked in windows, gone through garbage, or invaded her house, he hadn't admitted it. More than likely, her life had been so pathetically barren, he hadn't bothered to do more than follow her around. She'd never noticed him. She'd probably smiled at him, maybe served him dinner, sat by him in the movies, or discussed art with him at the gallery.

A sudden, brutal thought stunned her. He could be one of her friends. No. Cait refused to consider that idea. She might be too stupid and unobservant to notice a private detective following her, but she'd long ago learned to distinguish between friends and people who wanted to use her.

Not that it mattered who the detective was. He was merely a tool. Nausea rose in her throat. There could only be one reason for hiring a private detective to spy on her. Justin wanted evidence for a divorce case. Squeezing her eyelids tightly shut, Cait swallowed hard. Justin must believe she'd fight any divorce action. He wanted evidence he could use against her.

He must know by now there wasn't any. Maybe that was why Hank had pressured her to return to the ranch, but try as she might, Cait couldn't make sense of that. Outdoors, the clouds blotted out the sun, and a chill invaded the room. A truck passed, car doors slammed, Mrs. Courtney's voice sounded from the kitchen. Cait sat in thought. If she called the detective, he'd tell her nothing. Hank would tell her no more than he'd told her in the hospital.

As for Justin—pain ripped her heart. Justin didn't need any evidence. She'd told him she'd give him a divorce if he wanted one. There was only one thing she'd ever wanted from Justin Valentine. The dilemma now was whether to withdraw gracefully or to fight uselessly to the bitter end.

Nick rose and padded stiffly to her side. Poking her with his nose, he whined. Cait looked vacantly at him. Her head ached and her bottom was cold and sore from sitting on the vinyl-tiled floor. Nick whined again, this time gaining Cait's attention. "Oh, you want out, don't you?"

Struggling to her feet, she walked over to the door to the outside and opened it. Nick limped out. Shutting the door behind the old dog, Cait caught sight of herself in the small mirror beside the door. Her pupils were black and enormous, the blue irises reduced to thin circles.

Ghostly white skin stretched tight over high cheekbones. Her mouth was a grim slash of obscene color.

Cait started to turn away, but something about the face in the mirror drew her back. The random inheritance of genes. Her mother's eyes. Her grandmother's hair. Her great-grandfather's height. Her father's square jaw. Her father's stubbornness.

Rafe Montgomery never gave up. She'd heard it said so many times she'd come to believe it was her father's personal mantra. How could she have forgotten? Cait Valentine was Rafe Montgomery's little girl, and Rafe Montgomery's little girl always got what she wanted. Didn't she?

CHAPTER FOUR

CAIT walked back to the scattered papers on the floor. Her first compulsion to confront Justin gradually abated. If he knew she'd discovered the file of reports, he might accelerate his plans for divorcing her. She didn't want Justin to divorce her. She wanted him to love her. At least she thought she did. A Justin who hired a private detective to spy on her wasn't the Justin she loved.

Shaken by her discovery, Cait decided she needed more time to deal with her feelings, to deal with Justin's actions, to deal with everything. Was hiring a private detective to spy on a runaway wife more or less reprehensible than a wife running away? Her head ached too badly to answer that question now. She picked up the yellow file folder and stuck the papers inside, arranging the reports by date, as they'd been before, and carefully aligning the edges.

"What's so fascinating?"

Cait started. Lost in her thoughts, she hadn't heard Marilee walking through the dining room to the office. "I wouldn't call it fascinating." Cait played for time while her mind raced. Moving to the filing cabinet, she thrust the folder back where she'd found it. "Numbing is a better word. I've been sorting and filing papers for Justin for the past several centuries. I'm convinced Hank is allergic to discarding anything. I turned into a zombie hours ago." She looked at the large utilitarian clock on the wall. "I had no idea it was so late. If you're looking for Justin, he dumped all this in my lap and took off for parts unknown."

Marilee held up a cloth-wrapped bundle. "I brought some bread for Harry to serve with your dinner. I know how crazy Justin is about my homemade rye bread."

"How nice." Cait herded the other woman out of the office. "Only don't suggest Mrs. Courtney serve anything. After she fixes our dinner, she goes home. Justin and I serve ourselves, and I wouldn't dare suggest she make any additions or changes to her menu."

"She works for you, Cait," Marilee said. "You ought to be writing up a list of menus for her each week."

"Hank hired Mrs. Courtney as a housekeeper back when Marie was pregnant. She knows much better than I do what Hank and Justin like to eat."

"I'm sure you know best," Marilee said in a voice that clearly conveyed the exact opposite.

In the kitchen, the look Mrs. Courtney gave Marilee made Cait wonder how much of the conversation the housekeeper had heard. Leaning against a cabinet, Cait listened to Marilee expound on a recipe for bread and butter pickles she'd found that she was sure Mrs. Courtney would prefer to the one she currently used. Cait thought Mrs. Courtney's pickles were already better than gourmet quality, but she doubted the woman would appreciate her opinion so she kept quiet.

A small part of her found it cheering that even Mrs. Courtney couldn't meet Marilee's standards. Cait wondered if that had always been true and if she'd been too self-involved and self-pitying to notice it before.

Justin walked into the kitchen in time to hear Marilee's comment that she was sure Justin would prefer the new pickle recipe. "If Harry changes her pickle recipe—" he squeezed the housekeeper's shoulders in passing "—she's fired."

Cait bit the inside of her cheek to keep from laughing. She wanted to grab Justin by his shirt collar and give him a big kiss for taking the housekeeper's side. Then she'd like to grab the big iron skillet hanging by the stove and bang him over the head for being so low-down as to hire a private detective to spy on her. Her thoughts must have been reflected on her face because Justin gave her an inquiring look as he pulled a chair out from the table and straddled it.

"Was the paperwork that bad?" he asked in a commiserating voice.

"Yes." Worse than he knew.

"Justin, you should have told me you needed help in the office," Marilee admonished. "I would have been happy to make time to help you out."

"I appreciate your offer, but I wouldn't think of bothering you. I know how busy you are." Picking up the loaf of bread from the table, he sniffed deeply. "Rye."

"Your favorite." Marilee practically simpered.

If Cait hadn't glanced at Mrs. Courtney just then, she would have missed the way the housekeeper rolled her eyes. Odd, when one would have thought Marilee was a housewife after Mrs. Courtney's heart.

"Are you, Cait?" Justin asked.

"What?" She'd lost track of the conversation.

"Marilee said her back kills her after she's stood and kneaded bread all day, so she imagines you must be stiff and sore from leaning over the desk sorting papers. You do seem a little out of it. Were there any problems?"

"No, of course not." Unless one considered finding out one was married to a sneaking, spying husband was a problem. "Marilee's right. My shoulders are a little stiff."

"You need to try the hot tub after dinner."

"I saw you have one." Saw and wondered. In advertisements, hot tubs always held a couple—a man and a woman.

"Hank's been troubled with twinges of arthritis. He fought me tooth and nail on buying the tub, but after I threw him in it, he finally admitted it feels pretty good to old bones." Justin directed a frown Cait's way. "However, I don't want to catch Nick in there. Dog hair could really screw up the mechanics."

Marilee recoiled. "Ugh. Cait wouldn't let a filthy dog in there with her."

"Cait would let a horse in there if she thought it might make the horse feel better," Justin said dryly.

Marilee sighed. "I wish Lane and I had room for a hot tub. Of course we can't afford one, but some days I'd give anything to sit back and relax and play lady of leisure."

Cait clamped her jaw shut.

"You and Lane are welcome to use ours," Justin said. "Once Hank gets home he'll be in it a fair amount, I imagine, but now it pretty much sits unused."

Several hours later, stealing quietly down the stairs, Cait silently mimicked Marilee's profuse thanks at Justin's offer. Hopefully, Marilee would be too occupied spinning straw into gold to take him up on it very often. Marilee already wandered in and out of this house entirely too frequently to suit Cait.

Her hand gripped the railing as she came to a sudden stop on the staircase. Because the New House was ranch headquarters, Marilee considered little courtesies such as knocking unnecessary for family members, and she entered the house at will. Doubtlessly she also rambled through the entire house at will. And gloated in the knowledge that Justin had banned Cait from his bedroom.

Cait shook her head. The uncertain state of her marriage took precedence over Marilee's opinion. Cait padded the rest of the way downstairs and out to the sun-room, gasping as the cold floor tiles greeted her bare feet. Not bothering to switch on the lights, she dropped her robe on a chair and removed the cover from the hot tub. The warm water swirled around her as she stepped into the tub and sat on a submerged ledge.

The pulsing water massaged the tension from her muscles. She sank lower into the water and leaned her head back on the edge of the tub. The bulk of the ranch house shielded the sun-room from the glaring light in the ranch yard, leaving Cait in almost total darkness. A thin sliver of moon pointed to a bright star in a deep midnight-blue sky freckled with stars. To the west, the Sangre de Cristos rose as dark silhouettes, their snow-frosted peaks barely discernible. Her eyelids flickered shut.

"Want company?"

Water cascaded from Cait's body as she bolted upright. "I'm going to hang a bell around your neck," she said crossly, "if you don't quit sneaking up on me." She slid back down in the water. Her eyes had adjusted to the dark so she had no trouble watching Justin from beneath lowered lashes. Thankfully, he was wearing a swimsuit. Strong muscles molded arms, wide shoulders and a broad chest that led to a trim waistline and lean hips. In bed she'd loved measuring his long legs against hers. He'd won, of course, but the goal was not in winning but in feeling the rasp of masculine hairy legs rub slowly against hers. Need unfurled deep within her.

Justin settled inches from her and stretched out his legs. "Thanks for all the sorting you did. It was a big help. A couple of those bills were perilously close to being overdue."

The heat from his body swam through the water to caress her skin. Cait steadied her breathing. "Would you like me to file the stuff tomorrow?" His eyes were closed. Even in the dark she could see the thick lashes kissing his cheeks. His chest rose and fell slowly. She clasped her hands beneath her legs to keep her fingers from straying.

"I just finished taking care of it." He added, "I saw your camera this afternoon. Still taking pictures?"

"Yes." As if his little watchdog hadn't told him all about Cait's photography.

"Good." Lazily, Justin trailed his legs from one side of the tub to the other. They ended up barely touching Cait's legs. "Just checking," he said.

Cait held herself very still. "Checking?"

Justin chuckled. "To see if you had Nick hidden in here. I could have shot myself for telling you the hot tub was good for Hank's arthritis. You're such a pushover when it comes to animals."

"I am not," Cait said indignantly, turning toward him. She'd forgotten how close he was. His eyes were open, dark gleaming pools. Reaching up with a wet finger, she brushed one of his unruly eyebrows. Her finger slid down to the corner of his mouth.

Justin's large hand captured her finger, guiding it to the center of his mouth. His lips parted and he slowly sucked her finger inside. His teeth nibbled on the tip.

Moisture from the hot tub curtained the windows with condensation, isolating the two of them from the outside world. Cait's breathing drummed rapidly in her head. Or maybe the sound came from the pulsating water. Her finger tingled all the way to her naked toes. Cait couldn't drag her eyes away from Justin's intense gaze. An occasional whiff of the masculine-scented soap clinging to his skin drifted her way. She breathed his name.

It might have been a signal. Justin capped the back of her head with his hand and tugged her face nearer. With a deep sigh, Cait went willingly into his arms. He pulled her body onto his lap and slid them down so the water lapped over their shoulders, caressing their bodies even as Justin caressed her mouth with his lips. Her hands slid over silken wet skin, loving the warm strength beneath her fingertips. Justin deepened the kiss, his hands investigating the back fastenings of her swimsuit. He was going to make love to her, Cait thought with mounting pleasure.

"You smell good," Justin murmured against her lips. "It's enough to drive any man wild."

The words were too similar to the ones he'd said the night she'd come back when he'd claimed all he wanted from her was to satisfy his physical needs. Cait froze, then withdrew her mouth from his. "I suppose you'd say that to any woman who happened to be sitting in the dark in a hot tub while wearing a scanty bathing suit." When Justin didn't reply, she scrambled from his lap. He made no move to stop her. She huddled across the hot tub from him, her knees drawn up, her arms crossed in front of her to control her trembling.

Justin expelled a long breath. "I'm not sure what you want from me."

Love, she thought, but she couldn't give him that answer. Finally she said, "That makes us even, because I don't know what you want from me, either." The minute the words left her lips, she wanted to yank them back. What if Justin told her he wanted a divorce? The blood thundering in her ears drowned out his reply. "What?"

"I said we have company."

Cait heard the approaching voices. Having no desire to share the hot tub and make small talk, she hurriedly stood up and grabbed her robe, throwing it over her dripping body.

Marilee stopped in the doorway, Lane hovering behind her. "It looks like we had the same idea," Marilee said brightly.

Justin leisurely climbed from the hot tub and picked up his towel. "It's all yours."

Cait practically dashed from the room. Behind her, she heard Justin's last comment.

"We're through," he said.

Cold shivers racked her body. Through with the hot tub? Or through with each other?

"Here are all the instructions, the times, the temperatures, everything you need. I set the oven on automatic and stuck the roast in, so you don't need to do anything until it's time to put in the vegetables."

"Don't worry about a thing, Mrs. Courtney. This will be a big help." Cait waved the slip of paper at the middle-aged housekeeper. "You and Court enjoy your visit with your niece."

"If we leave here too late, the baby will be sleeping," Mrs. Courtney pointed out for the umpteenth time.

"What's the point in driving to Denver to see a brand-new great-niece if you can't hold her and check out her toes?"

"Exactly what Court said—" Mrs. Courtney frowned "—but are you sure you can manage? I should have made sandwiches or thawed hamburgers for Justin to cook. I don't suppose you want to invite yourselves to Marilee's for dinner."

"Definitely not. Go, go." Cait made shooing gestures with her hands. "If you don't hurry home and get ready, Court will start chewing nails." The housekeeper gave Cait one last doubtful look and reluctantly departed.

Cait grimaced. Poor Court. All the way to Denver he'd probably have to listen to his wife enumerate the reasons Justin shouldn't have married some rich girl from the big city. Cait looked down at the instructions Mrs. Courtney had handed her. The potatoes and carrots needed to be added to the roast around 5:00 p.m. Cait looked at the kitchen clock. The minute hand crept toward two. She had plenty of time.

Upstairs in the attic of the old farmhouse, Cait resolutely ignored mysterious trunks and boxes that looked as if they'd been there for decades. She itched to investigate them, but they'd have to wait until another time. Strings of outdoor Christmas lights had turned up in her search for the Christmas-tree decorations. When asked, Mrs. Courtney said that years ago Hank and Marie had strung the lights up every Christmas, but Hank had gotten out of the habit after Marie died. She'd added that the men hadn't celebrated Christmas much after Justin outgrew his teens.

Cait rested her hands on the box. No one needed to tell her Justin and Hank weren't much on Christmas. She blinked and shoved the memories aside. Justin and Hank were going to be very surprised when they saw the outdoor Christmas lights blazing from the trees and house.

She'd debated mentioning the lights to Justin and asking him for help, but several things held her back. The tree in the living room might not be everyone's idea of the perfect Christmas tree, but Cait loved every scrawny branch and every tattered decoration. Some of the ornaments, dating from Marie's grandparents, were probably sought by collectors. Cait's favorite was a lopsided, glue-smeared star made from drinking straws colored yellow. Justin had made the star when he was six years old, and Marie had saved it when she'd helped sort Justin's parents' household possessions after their deaths.

Taking Justin at his word that she could decorate a tree however she wanted, Cait had added a papier-mâché Santa created last year by her friend Sarah's daughter, Latisha, a Santa on horseback her friend, Dorie, had given her, and a patchwork angel Cait had bought at a Christmas bazaar because she knew Marie would have loved it. Thinking about the tree gave Cait great pleasure, but she hadn't forgotten Justin's ridicule of the "mythical" story of Marie's tree.

Then, too, the existence of the yellow file haunted her. The question of what to do about it—whether to fling it in Justin's face and demand an explanation or ignore it—kept her awake at nights.

And finally, her reluctance to ask Justin for help could be directly traced to the evening they'd spent in the hot tub. Since that night, Cait had made sure she soaked at times Justin was otherwise occupied. Cowardly, yes, but she didn't trust herself around him when both were half-naked with warm water sloshing over them. It wasn't that she didn't want to sleep with Justin, because she did. What was unbearable was the knowledge that while she'd be making love to Justin, he'd only be taking care of his physical needs with the nearest available female.

No, she wouldn't ask Justin for help. He thought the only thing she was capable of doing was warming a man's bed. Marilee made no effort to disguise her opinion that Caitlin Valentine was incapable of carrying out the simplest chore. Cait thought of Mrs. Courtney's detailed instructions for preparing dinner. Had it never occurred to anyone to wonder how Cait had eaten for the past two years? Obviously everyone in the entire Wet Mountain Valley believed she had the IQ of a discarded boot.

The box of lights was heavier than she'd anticipated, but Cait managed to haul it down both flights of stairs with minimum breakage. Fortunately, there were extra bulbs in the box. She started to shove the box outside, then remembered how she'd put the lights on the Christmas tree without checking the strings for burned-out bulbs. One bad bulb meant the entire string stayed dark, and it had taken her forever to figure out which bulbs were no good.

She pushed the box along the floor to an electrical outlet. Nick dogged her steps, sticking an inquisitive nose into the box. "It'll serve you right if a mouse is in there and bites you." The lights were wrapped around large squares of cardboard, facilitating testing and replacing broken and burned-out bulbs. Triumphantly, Cait sat back on her heels. "There. I'm not so hopeless. So what if I didn't learn all this housekeeping stuff in my cradle like everyone around here. Maybe that's something else in a person's genes. My mother wouldn't have a clue how to cook a roast. Oh, well. C'mon, Nick, let's get a ladder and stuff to nail these up. I'll do the trees first."

She should have known it wouldn't be that easy. How did one lean a ladder against an evergreen tree? Every time she started up the ladder, it pressed against the branches and slid to one side or the other. Trying to wedge the ladder between the branches and the tree trunk proved no more successful. Cait stood back and eyed the huge tree. She'd never climbed a tree, but this tree, while taller than the house, had thick, sturdy branches. Climbing it couldn't be much more difficult than climbing stairs. One just went from branch to branch. Thirty minutes later, her hands brown and sticky with tree goop, her hair a pincushion for pine needles, at least two red scratches on her face and who knew how many bugs and spiders down her jacket collar, Cait conceded the tree had bested her.

Undaunted, she determined to make a start on the house, stringing the lights along the edge of the roof. Cait backed up, her hands on her hips, and surveyed the house from top to bottom. Dwarfed by the surrounding mountains and the sprawling valley, the house had never seemed very large or tall. Until now. The roof suddenly looked awfully high up. Higher, in fact, than the ladder would reach. Refusing to admit defeat, Cait took a second look.

Since she'd never strung outdoor lights, maybe she ought to start small. The sun-room roof was fairly flat and only one story high. Stringing lights on it should be a piece of cake.

Detouring around Nick, who'd long ago fallen asleep on a sun-warmed patch of earth, Cait hauled the ladder over and propped it against the side of the sun-room. First she'd measure out how many strings of lights she needed, a chore quickly accomplished by laying the lights on the ground around the room. Armed with a hammer and a coffee can of large nails she'd found in the toolshed, Cait slung a couple of strings of lights over her shoulder and headed up the ladder.

The two giant evergreens flanking the front door, along with the tall ranch house, created a sheltered area. Their protection failed to extend to the roof of the sun-room, a fact Cait had not appreciated until she stood up and swayed at the impact of the cold wind roaring across the valley. Quickly she dropped to her hands and knees and debated postponing the decorating until the next calm day. No. If she carefully maintained a low profile, the wind wouldn't bother her.

Someone should have explained that to the wind, she thought wearily some time later. Gusts had burrowed icily beneath her jacket, howled painfully in her ears, ripped the strings of lights from her hands and twice bowled the can of nails off the roof to the ground. Fortunately, both times the lid had stayed firmly in place. Cait lost track of the number of trips she'd made up and down the ladder. Happily, one more string of lights would see the roof completely outlined.

She was climbing back on the roof with the last string when disaster struck. The wind knocked over the can of nails. Cait flung her body toward the rolling can in a futile effort to catch it, and her outstretched foot kicked the ladder. The can of nails beat the ladder to the ground. Her heart in her throat, Cait crawled to the edge of the roof and looked down. Nick barked up at her, and she breathed a sigh of relief. The good news was no injured dog and no broken windows.

The bad news was Cait stranded on the roof. Justin had driven off hours ago, and she had no idea where Lane and the ranch hands were. The high bedroom windows on the second floor of the house were beyond her reach. There was nothing she could tie a string of lights to. Not that the idea of shimmying down one of them held tremendous appeal. If only she had a flag to wave. If only Marilee would look out a window. If only Nick could raise the ladder.

Nick. Cait peered over the edge of the roof again. Nick's muzzle still pointed skyward. He barked at the sight of Cait's head. If only she knew where Justin was. Sending Nick to look for him was such a gamble. If Nick didn't find Justin, would the dog come home? Or would he keep searching until he was too tired to make it back? Justin said Nick didn't see as well as he once had. Cait glanced at the sky. A heavy cloud mass at the base of the Sangre de Cristos seemed to be heading this way. Snow? She couldn't send Nick on what might be a fruitless, if not dangerous, task. This late in the afternoon, Justin or someone would be returning to the home ranch any minute now.

Cait looked out over the valley. The only things moving were cows. Not a single vehicle raised dust along the roads. In the distance, lights sprang on in another ranch house. The skies to the west turned pink while overhead a jetliner traced a golden contrail. With the disappearance of the sun and its feeble illusion of warmth, a deep shadow blanketed the entire valley with a bone-numbing chill. At least the wind, seemingly content with the havoc it had wrought, had died down. Sticking her hands in her pockets and hunching down in her jacket collar, Cait wished for gloves and a hat.

Movement to the east caught her eye. Pronghorn antelope, three of them. With their keen vision, they probably saw her on the roof and thought she was crazy. Which was nothing compared to what Justin would think. He could add stringing outdoor decorations to the extremely long list of things Cait Valentine managed to mess up. A list headed by her marriage.

Down the valley, a cluster of lights signaled that the citizens of Westcliffe were going about their business. Cait envied them in their warm houses. Rubbing her arms to increase circulation, she wondered where Justin was. Stars popped up in the sky. No longer able to read her watch, Cait thought about her obituary and pitied poor Justin having to admit his wife had died of hypothermia while stringing up Christmas lights on their roof.

A pickup pulled into the yard and headed toward the barn. Jumping to her feet, Cait hollered and waved. The pickup pulled around behind the barn, out of sight. Dejection pressed down on her. Then the sound of the engine stopped, giving her hope.

Crawling to the edge of the roof, Cait cautiously looked over. "Nick? You still there?" The dog woofed in answer. "Go to the barn, Nick. Bring whoever's there back. To the barn, Nick, then back here." She tried to mimic the signals she'd seen Justin give the dog. Hopefully, Nick saw them. Hopefully, he understood he was supposed to herd someone over to the house. Scooting away from the roof's edge, she watched as the dog disappeared in the gathering gloom around the barn.

"Cait? Is that you up there?"

Cait scrambled to the edge of the roof. "Lane. Am I glad to see you."

"Marilee was sure she saw someone up there. She insisted a burglar was trying to break into the house. What are you doing?"

"I was putting up Christmas lights and I accidentally knocked the ladder down. It's not funny."

Laughing, Lane switched on the powerful light he carried and located the ladder. "Isn't Justin around?"

"Of course he is," Cait said sarcastically. "That's why I'm still up here freezing on the roof."

"Why'd you come back, Cait?"

For a moment, she was too stunned to answer. Finally she said, "This is hardly the time to discuss that."

Lane picked up the ladder and held it against his body. Standing several feet from the house, he caught Cait's face in the glare of his lantern. "Marilee's always going on how Hank stole my dad's share of the ranch, but if Hank hadn't bought Wylie's share, Wylie would have sold it to someone else."

"I'm sure you're right. Do you think you could move the ladder closer?"

Lane might not have heard her. "Hank was making sounds about his will when I saw him last in the hospital."

Cait stifled an urge to swear at Lane. "Hank's so ornery, he'll outlive us all."

"Marilee says you were buttering him up so he'd leave you something."

"I don't want anything of Hank's," Cait said testily, "so Marilee has nothing to worry about. Would you please move the ladder over here? I'd like to get down."

"I wouldn't blame you," Lane said. "There's nothing wrong with a little private enterprise. I'm sure having a good-looking chick like you visit him in the hospital brightened Hank's days considerably."

Cait couldn't decide whether to laugh or to throw the hammer at Lane. It was probably wiser to do neither. "Can you in your wildest imagination see Hank leaving me so much as a weed on this ranch? He thinks I'm the worst thing to hit this part of the country since the Ute Indians stopped raiding."

Lane laughed. "Hank's getting old. Anybody who doesn't appreciate your finer points must be blind." He set the lantern on the ground before resting the ladder against the side of the sun-room. "Come on down. I'll grab you so you don't fall." Propping his foot on the bottom rung of the ladder, he looked up.

"I don't need anyone to grab me." Especially her husband's cousin, she added to herself. Disliking Lane's standing so close to the ladder watching her descend, she hesitated.

"C'mon, Cait. I don't bite. Here." He picked up the lantern and backed several yards away. "See?"

She couldn't stay up on the roof all night. "You stay right over there, Lane Rutherford. I don't trust you one bit." She'd prefer going down the ladder facing him, but she'd probably fall smack on her nose. Awkwardly reversing, she found the top rung of the ladder with her toe and started down as rapidly as she could. Her back to Lane, by the time the noise of his footsteps registered on her, his hands were on her hips, ostensibly guiding her down. Darn him. Cait swung her elbow wildly backward, lost her balance, teetered in midair and fell. Her body took her rescuer's down with her. They landed in a heap, Cait on top.

"We have to quit meeting this way," Justin murmured.

"That was you in the pickup. Nick did get you."

"Why so surprised? Were you expecting the Lone Ranger?" Justin evidenced no desire to move. "Are you okay?"

Cait nodded.

"Why did you try to belt me this time?"

She had no intention of telling him she thought he was Lane. "You took me by surprise, and I lost my balance."

"I'm not sure I even want to ask the next question."

Cait shrugged as best as one could shrug when stretched out full length on one's husband's body, his arms wrapped around one's waist. "Putting up Christmas lights."

"Of course," Justin said gravely. "Christmas lights."

"It is December."

"You're absolutely right." His chest shook slightly.

"Go ahead and laugh before you injure yourself."

"Justin, Cait, what in the world are you two doing?" Marilee's voice was breathless from running. "When Lane didn't come back, I was worried something had happened."

"Cait was afraid to leave her perch on the roof," Lane said.

"I was not afraid," Cait indignantly denied.

"What were you doing on the roof?" Marilee asked, bewildered.

"It's December, Marilee," Justin said solemnly. "Cait was putting up Christmas lights."

"Cait was? Honestly, Cait, is there anything you can do without causing a disaster?"

Cait took instant umbrage. She might be an incompetent klutz who had no business on a ranch, but Marilee didn't have to rudely and constantly point out that fact to everyone in Colorado. Propping her arms on Justin's chest, Cait glanced up at the other woman. "Actually, there are one or two things I rather excel at." Hopefully, there was enough lantern light for Marilee to adequately see and appreciate the slow, sultry, extremely provocative smile on Cait's face as she looked down at her husband. "Isn't that so, Justin?"

Justin cleared his throat. "One or two."

CHAPTER FIVE

"I STILL don't believe it was necessary for you and Lane to redo every string of lights I put up," Cait grumbled. "They would have been fine." Looking over her shoulder as she walked through the open doorway into the house, she grudgingly admitted, "The lights do look great."

Justin closed the door behind them. "The haphazard way you attached them, it's a wonder they stayed up as long as they did."

"You men just can't admit a woman can do anything." She shrugged out of her jacket. "Those lights were perfectly—" An acrid odor hit her nose. "Oh, no!" Throwing her jacket toward the coatrack, Cait raced to the kitchen. Smoke poured from the oven. "The roast!" she wailed. "And I was supposed to put the vegetables in at five." Which, according to the wall clock, was over two hours ago. The roast now could easily be mistaken for a large hunk of charcoal. Cait switched off the oven and opened the back door.

"Even Marilee couldn't have fixed dinner while stuck on the roof." Justin followed her into the kitchen.

"Marilee never would have gotten stuck on the roof," Cait said glumly, using a kitchen towel to wave smoke toward the open door. Determined to prove a little thing like a destroyed dinner couldn't get her down, she added, "If you don't mind waiting thirty minutes or so, I can make us some egg salad sandwiches."

"I hate egg salad," Justin said absently, poking at the roast. "This might not be too bad if you trim off the burned sides. We could probably salvage enough for hot meat sandwiches.''

''You hate egg salad?'' Cait asked slowly.

''Detest it. Always have, I... Damn.'' He gave her a crooked smile. ''Put both feet, boots, ankles and knees in it that time, didn't I?''

''You always told me you liked my egg salad sandwiches.''

''Hell, Cait, it's the only thing you know how to cook. What was I supposed to say? I wouldn't have said anything now if I'd been thinking.''

''You hate my egg salad sandwiches, but never said anything so you wouldn't hurt my feelings?'' At Justin's wary nod, she started giggling. ''I must have made them once a week.''

''At least,'' he said with a great deal of feeling.

Cait's giggles turned to full-blown laughter.

She smiled, thinking about it as she snuggled under her covers several hours later. Before, she'd been so busy demanding the big gestures, she'd missed the little ones. Forcing Justin to choose between going to the movies with her or finishing up the haying had been juvenile and doomed to failure. What she'd really wanted was Justin's spending more time with her. And when he did, she'd wasted that time by complaining how unhappy and abandoned she felt on the ranch. If only she'd known about the egg salad sandwiches. Maybe it didn't compare with a dozen red roses.... Maybe it meant more.

Her bedroom door opened. The hallway was dark, but enough light filtered in from outside to silhouette the man standing in the doorway. ''Justin?''

He strolled to the edge of the bed and looked down at her. ''About those one or two things you excel at...''

''Yes?'' Anticipation shimmered through her body.

''I'd like a demonstration.''

Cait inched across the mattress, making room for Justin to slide in beside her. "It's the least I can do," she murmured, "to make up for all those egg salad sandwiches you ate."

Tripping lightheartedly down the staircase, Cait smiled at nothing at all. Last night had given her more than pleasure. It had given her hope. Justin had not only taken in stride a burned roast and his wife's getting herself stranded on the roof, he'd come to her bed. Nothing had been said about Cait being the nearest available woman. Admittedly, nothing had been said about love, either, but two weeks still remained until their anniversary. Justin hadn't kicked her out of the house; last night he'd come to her bed. And even when they weren't between the sheets, for almost two weeks they'd managed to act in a perfectly civilized fashion toward each other. Life had never seemed so promising.

In fact, Cait felt so encouraged about the state of her marriage she'd decided to ask Justin to explain why he'd had a private investigator following her in Colorado Springs. He would have a perfectly good reason for his actions, and she could dismiss the whole matter from her mind.

Country music blared down the hall from the kitchen. Mrs. Courtney was a rabid fan. Cait hated nasal voices and hokey words, but she had to admit that sometimes the tunes were kind of catchy. Like now, she thought, finding herself humming along with a song about a cowboy who wanted to rid himself of a cantankerous woman.

She crossed the dining room to the office. Justin had left her bed before she awakened, and he usually ate breakfast at the Courtneys' so she hadn't seen him this morning. With luck, he'd be in the office phoning in orders or paying bills. When they were first married, she'd nibbled his ears and distracted him with kisses, trying to wheedle him into abandoning his chores and responsibilities for the day. If he refused, she'd cried and carried on and refused to speak to him for days. He'd expect that this morning. He wouldn't expect her to wish him good-morning and hand him the yellow file.

Justin wasn't in the office.

Neither was the file. Cait tore through the drawer. Then, starting at the top of the filing cabinet, she slowly, thoroughly, searched every drawer, every file folder. The yellow file was gone. Standing up slowly, she carefully studied the office, looking for any place the file could be.

A painstaking investigation of the chairs, the table, the floor and the desk came up empty. The reports from the private detective had disappeared. Cait sat numbly in the office chair. Justin had remembered the file and removed it. He didn't want Cait to see it. Should she tell him she already had?

Leather creaked, metal jingled and hooves clopped as Rosie plodded along the road. Someone sometime had said something about life looking better from the back of a horse. Cait wasn't sure it rang true, but healthwise, riding a horse beat pigging out on chocolate as a cure for depression. "Course, if I'd been smart enough to bring a candy bar, I could have done both." Rosie pricked her ears in the direction of Cait's voice; the ambling horse was a good listener. "If I wasn't such a coward, I'd ask Justin why he took the file."

A crow flew overhead, cawing raucously before spiraling down to join three buddies feasting on a dead rabbit. Cait nudged Rosie into a trot, scattering the large black birds. Crows had to eat, and scavengers cleaned up the countryside, but Cait preferred rabbits to crows. She didn't look back. The crows would have already returned. Chasing them off was temporary; her action changed nothing.

Cait's thoughts bounced back to Justin and the file. He could have removed it because he didn't want her to get upset that he'd had her followed. Which meant he wanted her to stay. Or...he might still be planning on divorcing her. Except surely the man who forced egg salad down his throat so as not to hurt her feelings wouldn't climb into her bed if he intended to boot her out of his house. Would he?

Having passed the pasture holding the bulls, Cait guided Rosie toward the orange gate to the next pasture. Leading the mare through, Cait fastened the gate behind her and remounted. Most of the cows strung along a ragged line of greenish hay ignored the passing rider. The hay smelled better than the cows. A couple raised their heads, chewing their cuds as they watched her apprehensively circle widely around them.

She exited through a gate into another pasture, relieved to find it empty of cattle. The route she'd chosen to reach the hills detoured around the pasture holding the bulls. One thick-necked bull watched her from the other side of the fence. A good, stout fence with a chained, locked and bolted gate, Cait devoutly hoped.

It was too bad sweet little baby calves grew up into these ungainly, big-footed, ugly, unappealing animals. Justin used to tease her that she'd never have married him if she'd known ranchers came with cows. She'd known it. She just hadn't known how much of a rancher's life revolved around cows.

One of many things she hadn't known. Still didn't know. If only she'd spent more time her first year of marriage looking beyond a heart-stopping smile, smoky green eyes and a knee-weakening masculine physique. She didn't know how Justin voted, if he wanted children and if so how many, if he'd ever wanted to be anything but a rancher...

She did know what he wanted in a wife. The moment when she'd unwrapped the book he'd given her for Christmas would be forever burned into her brain. A sort of guidebook for being a rancher's wife. With recipes included. Cait gave a small snort, half laugh and half sob. She'd bet there weren't any recipes for egg salad in the book.

Their first Christmas together and the book and a pair of flannel pajamas had been her only Christmas gifts from Justin. Hank hadn't given her anything. She'd showered them both with gifts, most of which she'd sensed were wrong the minute the men unwrapped them. The overriding emotion that Christmas morning had been embarrassment. Followed by hurt feelings. Cait didn't even want to think about her wedding anniversary, which had *not* been celebrated two days later.

The crusted snow crunched beneath Rosie's feet as the mare picked her way along a small stream. Ice rimmed the banks, in some places spanning the water. Small tracks decorated one such snow-covered bridge. Cait reined Rosie in. The tracks looked like the footprints of a cat. A very small cat. Leaning down from her saddle, Cait studied them as they led along the bank on the near side of the stream.

Straightening up, she made a cursory survey of the surrounding area. The nearest homestead was a long distance away, and the tracks were extremely small. Maybe they weren't cat tracks at all, but some kind of large mouse or rat. Or maybe someone living elsewhere had dumped unwanted kittens in the valley, figuring a rancher or farmer would take them in. More likely the kittens would become a coyote's dinner.

Almost unconsciously, Cait had been guiding Rosie along the cat's trail. Up ahead, a bald eagle sat in a half-dead tree near the creek bank. The large bird's head gleamed snowy white in the afternoon sun as he intently focused on a small thicket of willowy shrubs. The animal tracks led directly to the thicket. Cait let out a yell and Rosie leaped in the raptor's direction. The eagle turned his majestic head, glared at them and lifted himself into the sky with a lazy flapping of his long wings. His white tail flashed in the sun.

Cait brought Rosie to a sliding halt. Jumping from the mare, Cait dropped the reins to the ground and cautiously approached the small thicket. Failing to see any animal, she circled around the shrubs. No tracks emerged from the thicket. The animal was still inside. Cait dropped to her knees. "Here, kitty, kitty," she called softly. Nothing. She scooted closer and bent down to the ground. Scrunched in a pile of wet, moldy leaves at the base of the bushes, a tabby kitten looked almost dead. Only his trembling gave him away.

"You poor baby," Cait crooned. "How long have you been out here?" Reaching slowly in, she grabbed the tiny animal. Too weak and frozen to resist, the kitten gave one pitiful meow. Backing away from the thicket, Cait stood up and, holding the kitten in one hand, managed to remove her jacket and flannel shirt. Shivering as the cold air hit her bare skin, Cait quickly wrapped the shaking creature in her shirt, fashioned a sling from the sleeves and hung the bundle around her neck in front of her. She carefully zipped her jacket around the two of them. The kitten made no protest. "I hope we're not too late."

A loud snort answered her. Cait wheeled. Rosie held her head high while her ears flicked furiously. Cait looked in the direction of Rosie's wide-eyed stare, and her stomach plummeted to her toes. Trotting over a slight rise of ground, headed in her direction, was the biggest, meanest-looking bull Cait had ever seen. "It's okay, Rosie," Cait said quietly, hoping the mare wouldn't hear terror in her voice. She moved slowly toward the horse. Her foot landed on a brittle twig. The sharp snap sounded like a gunshot, and Rosie took off in a thundering of hooves, her tail flying high. The bull stopped, his massive head swinging toward the fleeing mare.

The head turned back in Cait's direction. She'd never seen such evil eyes. She backed up, looking wildly around for help. The stick near her feet would be a toothpick to this monster. A short distance away, several trees skylined the horizon. Maybe if she moved slowly... The bull kept pace. Cait speeded up. The bull broke into a slow trot. Cait turned and ran for her life.

The lowest branches were farther from the ground than she'd realized, but panic gave her strength. She clawed and grabbed and dug in with her toes, climbing until she'd reached the upper branches where the limbs grew so small she dared go no farther.

The bull stopped at the base of the huge tree and looked skyward, panting vast clouds of vapor. The sun gleamed off the ring in his nose.

Rosie stood on the far side of the pasture, facing Cait's refuge, her whole body exhibiting alarm. Each time the mare flung her head, her trailing reins flipped in the air. What a great time to discover Rosie hadn't been trained to be ground-tied, Cait thought morosely.

An eternity later, Cait gave up trying to find some portion of her anatomy that wasn't sick and tired of sitting in the crook of this tree, at the base of which the bull maintained a vigil. If Cait moved so much as an eyelash, he glowered up at her. About all he hadn't done was paw the ground and attack the tree.

The mare occasionally snorted and stamped the ground but kept her distance. If Rosie was a jumper, she'd have been back at the barn by now, and someone would come searching for her rider. Not for the first time, Cait regretted leaving Nick behind.

The kitten lay still against her chest. Reluctant to disturb him, Cait prayed he was sleeping. She tried to distract herself by thinking of names for the kitten.

A horse and rider coming at a fast lope crested the small rise. No one sat a horse like Justin did. Sometimes it was hard to tell where the horse stopped and the rider started.

Justin reined Nighthawk in below the branch Cait was perched on. "Bird-watching?"

"What else?"

"You hurt? Rosie throw you?"

"No and no."

Justin pointed Nighthawk toward the bull. In other circumstances, Cait would have enjoyed the performance. Justin rested his hands on his saddle horn and the black gelding did the rest. In minutes, Nighthawk had the bull trotting back over the hill. Cait started to descend, thought about it, then remained where she was. She wasn't sure, but it might be possible that even a cutting horse trained by Justin could lose a cow.

Justin returned without the bull. Nighthawk's presence calmed Rosie, and the mare allowed Justin to grab her reins and lead her over to the tree. Dismounting, Justin looked up. "You spending the night up there?"

"No." Cait scooted down the tree.

Justin caught her as she dangled from the lowest branch. "How the hell did you get up there?"

"Fear is a powerful motivator," Cait retorted.

"He was probably more curious than anything else."

"If you say so. I'm just happy you happened to be riding this way."

"Harry called down to the barn and said you'd been gone a long time. She was worried you were in some kind of trouble."

Cait sighed. It was difficult to argue about one's competency when one had spent the past several hours being terrorized by a stupid male cow.

Justin waited until they were in the saddle and headed back to the ranch house before he attacked. "Damn it, Cait, you ought to know better than to leave a gate open. I know you hate cows and ranching, but I thought we'd managed to pound the importance of closing gates into that city head of yours." He barely paused for breath. "Or did you deliberately turn loose that bull, and the trick backfired on you? I suppose I neglected to do or say something this morning, so this was your idea of revenge."

The anger in his voice dealt an almost physical blow, and Cait barely managed not to sway in the saddle. "I closed the gate. The bull must have been in the pasture, but I didn't see him."

"He wasn't in here," Justin said flatly. "I saw him with the rest of the bulls this morning when I fed them. You left the gate open."

"I didn't. I couldn't have." Justin's hat shielded his eyes and his thoughts from her. "I didn't even come through the pasture with the bulls. I don't like to ride past them." She reined in the mare and pointed. "I came along the road and then through that pasture and that one."

"Then how did Fred get through the gate?"

"Fred?"

"He's registered under some name as long as your arm, but we call him Fred," Justin said impatiently. "Don't change the subject."

"Maybe you left the gate open when you fed the cows this morning."

"I don't leave gates open."

"Neither do I." It was obvious he didn't believe her, and she refused to speak to him the rest of the way back. Movement beneath her jacket reminded her she carried a passenger. Dismounting near the corral, Cait led the mare to the man standing there. "Court, would you do me a favor, please, and take care of Rosie? I have a small problem I have to see to."

Spinning on her heel, she totally ignored Justin, who'd stalked up behind her. As Cait headed toward the house, she heard his voice by the barn issuing terse instructions. She walked faster.

In the empty kitchen, Cait unzipped her jacket. Growing restive, the kitten had almost managed to climb out of the shirt, but his tiny claws had become entangled in the fabric and he struggled to get free. "Calm down, little guy. I'll get you loose in a minute," she said gently.

Justin marched into the kitchen, slamming the door behind him with a bone-jarring crash. The kitten dug his hind claws into Cait for leverage and catapulted through the air, landing on the kitchen floor. In a flash, the tiny animal disappeared into the thin slot between the refrigerator and cabinet.

"What the hell was that?"

"A starving, half-frozen little kitten, whom you probably scared half to death," Cait said tartly. "Talk about my throwing tantrums." Ignoring the burning pain down her chest, she squatted down on her hands and knees to coax the kitten out.

"Where did you get a cat?"

"Someone must have abandoned him. I found him in the pasture as an eagle was considering him for dinner."

"That's why you got off Rosie," Justin guessed.

"Yes, and I did not open that gate." Wiggling her fingers, she slowly edged her hand into the dark slot. "Come on out, kitty. I won't let the big bad man hurt you. Ouch." She jerked her hand back, a hand now graced with two long red scratches. "Ungrateful little beast," she said softly. "Come on out, and Cait will feed you."

"Leave him. I'll put out some water and a little canned tuna. If he's hungry, he'll come out." When Cait stood up, Justin lifted her hand and frowned at the scratch. "Go up and wash that hand really good so it doesn't get infected. And I mean scrub it with soap and water. No telling what kind of filth is on that cat's claws. Maybe I should scrub it."

"No, I'll take care of it. You feed little kitty here." Holding her jacket closed, Cait headed upstairs to the bathroom. Safely inside, she removed her jacket. Six tiny holes punctured her skin above the center of her bra while two lines of red scored one breast above the nipple. Where her breast didn't burn, it throbbed like crazy. Cait discarded her clothes on the floor and stepped into the shower. By the time she'd finished soaping and scrubbing, her whole body felt like it was on fire, but she hoped the wounds had been sufficiently cleaned.

Justin walked into the bathroom as she stepped out of the shower. The towel came up an instant too late. "Why didn't you tell me that damned cat scratched you there?" he asked angrily, yanking down the towel.

Cait yanked the towel back up. "Go away. I'm trying to dry off before I freeze to death."

"Go ahead." He uncapped the tube in his hand.

"I'd like some privacy."

"And I'd like some dinner, so quit stalling." He grabbed her robe off the hook and handed it to her. "Put this on."

Deliberately turning her back to him, Cait shrugged into the heavy red robe and belted it snugly around her waist. She wrapped a towel turban-style around her hair.

"Give me your hand." Justin squeezed a dab of salve on his finger and waited expectantly.

"I cleaned it thoroughly."

"This is disinfectant. Just in case." He reached for her hand, inspected it, then gently smeared the medication over the scratches. He reached for the tube again.

"I'll do the rest," Cait said hastily, clutching the edges of her robe together.

Justin squeezed more medication onto his finger. Brushing aside her hands, he slid open her robe, exposing the angry red marks. "He really nailed you."

Cait caught her breath as Justin's fingertip soothed the cooling salve over her skin.

"Does it burn?"

"No." Not the way he meant. Embarrassed by the rapid rise and fall of her chest as he treated her wounds, she closed her eyes. Justin couldn't help but notice the effect he was having on her. Her breathing speeded up and grew shallower as his finger approached the tip of her breast. The heat from her skin instantly melted the cool salve. Unable to trust her trembling knees to support her, Cait reached back with one hand to brace herself against the cabinet. Her breast throbbed from more than pain, and she knew the nub must be hard and pointed. Justin's finger grazed the tip, eliciting a gasp from Cait. Her eyelids fluttered open as his hand stilled.

"Did I hurt you?" he asked in a hoarse voice.

Cait shook her head, her eyes locked on his middle shirt button. "It's fine, thank you." She sounded as if she'd just run a marathon.

"This is new." Justin flicked the horseshoe charm hanging around her neck. "You always seem to wear it."

"It was a gift from a friend." Dorie had given it to Cait the last time Cait had tutored her. For good luck, Dorie said.

"Not your usual style."

He meant the charm was an inexpensive trinket. "Dorie doesn't have a lot of money, but she's been a good friend."

Justin closed her robe and firmly tied the belt. "Keep a close eye on those scratches. Infection could still set in." His voice was back to normal.

She wanted to suggest he keep an eye on them. Instead, she meekly agreed to watch the scratches and asked about the kitten.

Justin laughed. "Dry your hair and come see for yourself."

Nick lay on his bed in the corner of the kitchen. Curled up against the dog was a little gray-striped furry ball. The kitten's bulging stomach attested to his having eaten well. Cait laughed. "Nick's adopted him."

Justin pulled a casserole from the oven. "I think it's the other way around. And I think he is a she, which is probably why she got dumped. I doubt she's two months old."

"Poor baby." Cait set plates and silverware on the table. "I was going to name him Lucky, but if she's a girl..." She thought a minute. "How about Lucy?"

"I suppose," Justin said in a resigned voice, "that means you've adopted her." He sat down across the table.

"What did you expect me to do with her? Take her over to De Weese Reservoir and toss her in?"

"Knowing you, I expected you to adopt her," he said amicably.

"I will check around to see if anyone's trying to find Lucy, in case she wandered off or something." Holding her fork in the air, Cait observed the animals. "Isn't she darling?"

Justin gave himself a second helping. "She's a cat."

Cait laughed. "I heard you sweet-talking her as I went upstairs, you old softy, you."

"No doubt Marilee's right. I overindulge you," he said, a deadpan expression on his face. "My big mistake was not training you right when I brought you here."

She made a face at him. "Speaking of training, there are a few gaps in Rosie's training. She apparently wasn't taught to stand ground-tied, and I've never seen one of your horses spook like that around a cow, not even a bull. She can't be much use to you as a cow pony."

"The man who bought her didn't run a spread. His wife rode Rosie for pleasure."

"Why did you buy her back? For her foals?"

"I didn't think it'd matter to you whether or not she was trained as a cow pony, the way you feel about cows."

Justin left to answer a ringing phone before Cait could get her gaping mouth to form a question. Waiting for Justin, she cleared away the dishes and cleaned the kitchen, his words continuously replaying in her head. Justin couldn't possibly have purchased the mare specifically for Cait because he'd learned of Cait's return to the ranch only days before she came back. Court said the mare had been at the ranch for over a year.

She'd ask Justin what he meant. After hanging up the wet kitchen towel, Cait headed for the office. She could hear Justin's voice behind the closed door. From the one-sided conversation, it was evident Justin was talking to Hank. Switching directions, she went into the small room that held the TV. Justin never emerged from the office, and after watching the late news, Cait gave up waiting for him, flipped off the TV and went to bed.

Floundering in the crusted, thigh-high snow, she looked back. The bull was gaining on her. Despite his gargantuan size, he had no trouble skimming along the white surface. Marilee's mocking face appeared beside Cait. Marilee, too, bounded lightly over the crust. "Ranch wives know the secret."

The words came, not from Marilee's mouth, but from above. Cait looked up. A bald eagle with Lane's face leered down from his perch in a tall tree. Cait changed course, heading for the tree. The tree skipped away, its roots tiptoeing gaily atop the snow. Only Cait plunged through the cold, biting surface with each desperate step. The bull snorted in her ear, his hot breath searing her face. Horns, eight feet long, ripped into her. Pain slashed across her chest, but Cait struggled on. Atop a hill, a man sat on a black horse. She yelled at him. He didn't see or hear her. Cait screamed her husband's name again. And again.

"Cait! Wake up!"

Cait opened her eyes. Justin sat on the edge of her bed, leaning over her. "I must have been dreaming," she said.

"You scared the hell out of me. The way you screamed my name, I thought you were being murdered."

"A bull was chasing me through the snow. I was so cold and I couldn't get away." She trembled, unable to completely cast off the emotional dregs of the dream. "He had long horns and he kept digging into my chest and it hurt so bad."

"Your chest?" Justin frowned. "Let me see." He switched on the lamp beside the bed.

Cait clutched at her covers. "It was just a dream."

"A dream in which you felt pain." He firmly moved aside her hands. "Those scratches could be infected." Quickly he unbuttoned her flannel pajama top and edged it open. "They look okay, but we'll keep an eye on them."

The next thing Cait knew, she'd been bundled off to Justin's darkened bedroom and deposited in the center of his bed.

Justin climbed in beside her. "A man can't get a decent night's sleep on the mattress in that room," he said. "Tell Harry to order a new one."

She waited for him to reach for her, but he made no move to bridge the slight distance between them. Cait wondered if he'd recognized her flannel pajamas. She'd never seen the pajama bottoms he was wearing. During the first year of their marriage, he'd slept nude. She looked at him. Bare skin sweeping across wide, muscled shoulders gleamed in the dark. She stretched out her hand. His back warmed the tips of her fingers.

"Go to sleep, Cait." His voice was harsh.

She jerked back her hand. Justin didn't want to make love to her. His need for her, for the nearest woman, no longer existed. Soon he'd tell her to leave. She thought of the missing file, the private detective reports that had disappeared. She would ask him about them now. She meant to ask him. Entirely different words came from her mouth. "When you came to New York, if we hadn't slept together, would you have asked me to marry you?"

The silence lasted so long she was about to repeat the question when Justin answered in a voice so low Cait strained to hear him.

"No," he said.

Somewhere in the distance, a dog barked a sharp warning. Cait held her body still, willing the pain to go away. Not the surface pain from the kitten's scratches, but a deeper pain. Excruciating pain no medication could ever reach or heal.

CHAPTER SIX

CAIT woke up with a nose full of fur and sneezed.

Justin laughed. "Nick isn't the only one Lucy's adopted."

She forced open eyelids heavy with sleep. Small feline eyes stared back at her from inches away. "Where'd you come from?"

"You don't remember hauling her home?" Justin asked.

"Yes." Memories awakened Cait with a vengeance. She remembered more than the kitten. She remembered she was in the bed of the man who regretted marrying her. Safety lay in talking about the kitten. "I wondered what she was doing up here."

"Looking for you. How are the scratches?"

"Fine."

"Fine, as in you don't even notice them, or fine, as in you're not about to let me look?" he asked dryly.

Cait lifted her gaze from the kitten. "Both."

Completely dressed, Justin sprawled on the bed, his head propped on a bent arm. His other hand gently scratched the kitten. "If I said I intended to look anyway?" he asked softly.

"I'll set Lucy on you."

Justin grinned. "Is this a case of like adoptive mother, like kitten? A man could go crazy wondering if he's liable to get purring or sharp claws."

Cait ran her fingers over the kitten's soft fur. "She's nice to anyone who's nice to her."

He reached for Cait's scratched hand. "Remind me why she gave you this. Were you beating her?"

"You frightened her."

Justin snorted and rolled off the bed. "I can see what a timid kitty she is, the way she strolled in here and made herself at home on my bed." He opened a dresser drawer and searched through the contents.

Was he referring to the kitten? Or to her? Cait sought frantically for something to say to fill what was becoming an awkward silence. Bringing up the missing file or asking him why he'd bought Rosie were not options. Last night had taught her the dangers of asking questions whose answers she might not like. Finally she said, "I thought I heard you talking to Hank last night. Yesterday morning he told me he was waiting to hear when he could come home. Does he know yet?"

"Monday, which works out great." Justin tucked a handkerchief in his back pocket and headed for the bedroom door. "There's a charity bash up in the Springs Saturday night, so break out the glad rags. We'll go up Saturday after morning chores and spend the weekend at the hotel, then bring Hank back with us on Monday." He walked out of the room.

Happiness cascaded over Cait. Justin had said "we" and "us". He wanted her to go with him. This must be the same charity ball they'd attended two years ago. She remembered the party—the men in tuxes, the ladies in fancy dresses. The bottom dropped from her world. Fancy dresses. She couldn't go to a ball. Scooping Lucy up in one hand, Cait raced from the bedroom. Justin stood at the bottom of the staircase talking to Marilee. Cait hung over the railing. "Justin, I can't go to a formal dance. I don't have anything to wear."

"Hell, Cait, you have more fancy dresses than we have cows."

"Actually," she said diffidently, "I don't. Not really. Not anything suitable."

"You don't need the latest designer outfit from New York. Whatever you have hanging in your closet will be fine."

"That's just it," Cait said. "There isn't anything hanging in my closet. I, uh, left my party dresses in Colorado Springs."

"In one of those storage units, I suppose. Don't worry about it. We'll get there in plenty of time for you to fetch what you need from storage."

"Well, uh, you see, I didn't store them. They aren't exactly mine anymore."

"You gave all your dresses away?" Justin asked in disbelief.

"That's one way to get new clothes. I wish I was half as clever at getting something out of my husband," Marilee said in admiration. "I'm stuck wearing the same old rag I wore last year."

"Last year?" Cait clutched at the railing. Justin had been in Colorado Springs last year and he hadn't bothered to call or come see her.

"Lane and I went with Hank. Ol' Stick-in-the-Mud Justin stayed home."

Justin ignored Marilee's playful remark. "I don't want to argue about the party, Cait. You can buy a new dress in Colorado Springs, but you're going."

Cait bristled. "Is that an order, Justin?"

Justin put on his hat, shoving it to the back of his head as he looked up at Cait. A slow grin crawled across his face. "You know, Mrs. Valentine," he drawled, "I believe it is. Wanna make something of it?"

Darn Justin and his smiles. It was fortunate Cait was hanging on to the banister because her knees were useless for holding her up. "I wouldn't think of it, Mr. Valentine," she said breathlessly.

"Cait, what in the world have you got there?" Marilee demanded. "It looks like a cat."

"Meet the newest member of the family," Justin said.

"I suppose Cait drug him home."

"He's a she," Cait said. "Her name is Lucy."

Marilee shook her head. "Harry won't be happy. Cats get into everything, and it's impossible to train them."

"Then she'll fit right in," Justin said, "with all the other untrainable females around here."

Cait immediately fired up. "I told you, Justin, I did not leave that cattle gate open."

"Cait, you didn't leave open a gate and let out some cattle?" Marilee shook her head reprovingly.

"She didn't," Justin said, "but someone did."

"If one was open..." Marilee shrugged. "Cait might mean well, but let's face it, Justin, she's a walking disaster on a cattle ranch."

It was impossible to refute Marilee's statement. The kitten meowed in protest as Cait inadvertently squeezed the small animal.

"Cait said she didn't do it and I believe her. If she'd left the gate open, she'd own up to it."

"Well, of course, if you choose to believe her, then there's nothing more to be said." Marilee looked up at Cait. "I'll be happy to help you select a suitable dress on Saturday."

"Thank you, but that won't be necessary." Cait smiled sweetly down at the other woman. "I may not know anything about ranching, but when it comes to shopping, I'm one of the best."

"I suppose your new friends in the Springs will shop with you," Marilee said. "You ought to invite them to the dance." The suggestion came across as a challenge.

"That's a good idea. Why don't you, Cait?" Justin asked.

"It's not the sort of thing they'd enjoy. Or be able to afford."

"Maybe Cait's too embarrassed to introduce her friends to us." Marilee's smile revealed sharp little teeth.

"Certainly not," Cait said instantly. "As Hank would say, the three of you clean up real good. You wouldn't embarrass me at all. Besides, my friends are very tolerant." Marilee's smile faltered. Satisfied, Cait looked at Justin, who was staring thoughtfully up at her. "If you'd like to meet them," she said in a deliberately casual voice, "I think it would be fun for them if you treated them to brunch at the hotel on Sunday. It's sort of beyond their budget."

"All right. I'll make the arrangements. How many?"

"Four, besides us," Cait said.

Justin walked to the front door and held it open. "I believe I caught you on the way out, Marilee." Lane's wife sailed through the doorway. Justin raised his head and winked broadly at Cait.

"Justin, wait." Cait ran down several steps. "I want, that is... Thank you for believing me about the pasture gate."

"I owe you an apology for not believing you from the beginning. It's no excuse, but I was worried about you, and when I saw you were okay, I lashed out. If I'd bothered to calm down and think about the situation for half a second, I'd have realized you would have admitted immediately you'd screwed up." He paused. "And I was wrong to accuse you of deliberately letting the bull out. You're capable of a lot of things when you don't get your way, but you'd never be malicious or destructive." His voice flattened. "I know I can trust you."

Cait blinked suddenly damp eyes. "Thank you, Justin."

"You might consider trusting me—" Justin gave her an enigmatic look "—and tell me why it's important you stay until after Christmas." Tugging his hat low over his forehead, he walked out the door.

She couldn't tell him that. Not yet. Cait sat down on the staircase, a hundred and one disjointed thoughts and questions running riot through her brain. What gave Marilee the idea Cait wouldn't want Justin to meet her friends? Surely she didn't think Cait had a lover in the Springs. Cait's fingers froze on Lucy's head. Had Marilee suggested such a thing to Justin? Was that why he said he trusted her? She thought of the missing file. Justin had documented evidence proving Cait had not cheated on him with another man. Of course he trusted her.

She rose slowly to her feet and climbed the stairs to Justin's bedroom. Her husband didn't love her, wished he hadn't married her and had no interest in making love to her. All of which made it difficult to celebrate his trust in her. A trust based on the word of a hired stranger.

Shutting the bedroom door, Cait set Lucy down and threw herself full length on Justin's bed. At least Justin had believed her about the gate. It wasn't much to build on, but it was all she had. She felt a tiny thump as the kitten landed on the bed next to her. Reaching out with her finger, Cait stroked the kitten above her little pink nose and daydreamed about buying the perfect dress. A dress that would bring her husband to his knees. A dress that would drive him crazy. A dress that would make Justin fall in love with his wife.

A sharp pain stung the end of Cait's finger. The kitten had bitten her.

*   *   *

Justin's eyes gleamed as he shut their hotel room door. "You weren't kidding when you said you knew how to shop."

Lane and Marilee stepped into the hall from the room next door. Marilee inventoried Cait's appearance with a sweeping glance. "I hate to think how many cows we're going to have to sell to pay for that dress," she said tartly.

"If I have to sell the whole herd, it's worth every cow." Justin's eyes were warm with masculine appreciation.

Cait felt like floating. She flirtatiously fluttered her eyelashes at him. "I'll remember that the next time I want a new dress, because this one didn't cost you a single cow."

Justin pushed the elevator button. "Find a dress hidden in the back of your closet?"

"No." She stepped into the elevator. "My parents bought this dress."

"What the hell do you mean—" Justin followed the others "—your parents bought the dress?" The snarling question reverberated inside the wood-paneled elevator. "Did you tell them you needed a new dress?"

Cait gave him an uncertain smile. "Not exactly."

"Not exactly, meaning exactly what?"

Cait glanced at Lane and Marilee, who were avidly listening, their eyes bright with expectation.

Justin followed Cait's gaze. A muscle jumped in his cheek. "We'll talk about it later," he said stiffly.

Confused and embarrassed by Justin's anger, Cait turned to Marilee, praising the other woman's dress. "Your turquoise earrings match the color of the dress perfectly."

Marilee gave her a gloating smile. "They're an early Christmas gift from Lane."

Lane gave Cait a challenging look. "Can't have Marilee looking like a poor relation."

Justin cleared his throat. "Don't you have something to say to Cait, Lane?"

"Oh, yeah, sure," Lane said easily. "Sorry about the bull the other day, Cait. I never figured you to be off the mare or I'd never have played the trick on you." His grin invited her to share the joke.

Cait stared disbelievingly at him. "That was a trick?"

"Everyone knows you're scared spitless of the bulls. It was just a bit of harmless fun. After I opened the gate, I whipped back to the barn and made a bet with Terry that you'd come hightailing it back right behind me. I lost five bucks when you didn't." His gaze shifted to over her shoulder. "I didn't know until later you got stuck up the tree." He gave a little laugh. "Maybe I should have figured something like that would happen. After you got stuck on the roof and all."

It wasn't what Lane said so much as how he said it that told Cait he'd known darned well she was up that tree. If Lane was waiting for her to accept his so-called apology, he could wait forever. She turned her back to him.

The elevator door opened, and Lane and Marilee departed, Marilee's high heels tapping across the marble-tiled floor.

"Justin—" Cait began, stepping out into the lobby.

"Not now, Cait."

Cait pivoted on her heel and punched the elevator button. This family wanted no part of her. Well, that was perfectly fine with her. She wasn't about to beg them to like her, to accept her. The elevator was still there, and the door opened immediately. Cait marched inside and jabbed the button for their floor. She wasn't quick enough. The door closed, penning her inside the elevator with Justin.

"What the hell is this all about?"

"Not now, Justin," Cait spat, refusing to even look at him. Gone was the anticipation of a party. Evaporated away were the warm feelings of intimacy she'd felt sharing a hotel room with Justin, fixing his tie, stepping around him and bumping into him as they'd dressed. The elevator door opened, and she dashed out toward their room. Justin had the computer card that unlocked the door. Whirling, Cait held out her hand.

Justin opened the door and stalked over to the windows on the far wall. His back to her, he snapped, "Spit it out, Cait. Let's hear how I never buy you expensive jewelry like Marilee's earrings, that I give you stupid things like flannel pajamas. Damn it, you were always complaining about being cold. I notice you're wearing those damned pajamas for all you had to say about them two years ago."

As she stared wide-eyed at the stiff, defensive stance of her husband, Cait's anger deflated like a popped balloon. "You were right about the pajamas. They're warm and comfortable."

"And red. You wear red a lot, so I thought you'd like red pajamas."

Justin's words rendered Cait speechless. She'd have sworn he put more thought into how much orange juice to drink in the morning than he'd put into buying her a Christmas present.

Justin expanded on his grievance. "It's damned difficult to buy a present for someone who's been given everything she ever wanted all her life. What could I possibly give you that you don't already have?" He turned slowly to face her. "I couldn't give you Rascal.

She belonged to the ranch, not to me." He added flatly, "I wanted to buy you a dress for tonight."

"I thought you'd be pleased you didn't have to pay for it. My parents are going to Frankfurt, Germany over the holidays, and Mother's frantically busy getting ready. Since she doesn't have time to shop, she asked if she could send me a check, and I said yes, that I was planning to buy a new dress." Taking a deep breath, Cait locked her hands together and looked past Justin. "Everyone is always praising Marilee for being so economical, I wanted to show you I can be economical, too." She tried to smile. "Marilee's right. I screw everything up."

Justin shook his head. "Marilee's not right about you. She's just jealous." A look of chagrin passed across his face. "Like I was jealous of Lane. I knew he was giving those damned earrings to Marilee, and I thought about buying you something, but I was buying the dress, which you said you needed, and you have a jewelry box full of stuff you never wear." Drawing near, he brushed back the hair covering her ear. "I suppose these are from your folks, too. I doubt they're fake diamonds and pearls."

Suddenly, Cait understood what it meant to feel giddy. She gave Justin a warm, teasing smile. "Fake from Rafe Montgomery? Be serious." The lapels on his evening jacket felt smooth and cool beneath her palms. "My parents couldn't attend my high school graduation because they had to go to Hong Kong, so they gave me these." Her smile faded. "I'm sorry about the dress."

"I'm sorry I acted like such a jerk." He flicked a finger across her cheek. "Shall we try to go down to dinner again?"

Only if she could convince her boneless legs to move.

They had the elevator to themselves. Cait smiled shyly at Justin and wondered why men made such a fuss about wearing evening clothes. Justin in dusty blue jeans made her weak in the knees. Formally dressed in black and white, he weakened every joint in her body.

Justin pressed the button for the floor they wanted. "I like you in red."

His leisurely head-to-toe inspection stole her breath away. "Thank you," she managed. The red, ankle-length, form-fitting tube of heavy silk had been designed with a high neckline and tight long sleeves.

"But it seems to me, a truly economical wife would have gotten more material for her money." Pulling her to him, he slowly trailed his fingers over the large expanse of skin left exposed by the backless dress. "On the other hand—" his smile curled her toes "—no matter who paid for the damned thing, you look sexy as hell in it." His lips descended.

The elevator door opened. With heightened color, Cait allowed Justin to escort her past the interested couple waiting for the elevator. A choking sound came from Justin. Far from being embarrassed at being caught in an elevator in a heated embrace, her reprehensible husband was laughing.

Cait waited to get back at him until they stood in the doorway of the ballroom. Several couples looked their way and waved at Justin. As he started across the floor toward the table where Lane and Marilee were sitting, she stopped him with her hand on his arm. Standing on tiptoe, she whispered demurely in his ear, "I'm glad to know how much you like me in red because I brought my flannel pajamas."

There was only the slightest hesitation in Justin's step. His gray-green eyes glinted down at her. "I like you out of red even better. Have those damned cat scratches healed yet?"

*   *   *

The evening passed in a blur. The ballroom was elegant, the dinner divine, the speakers witty, the other guests charming and the music lively. Justin's smiles and the evocative hint of his clean-smelling scent set Cait's head awhirl. She was vaguely aware of elegant Christmas decorations, marble floors, tender beef and pink poinsettias on the tables. It would be impossible to remember all the people Justin introduced her to. Some she'd met before. None mentioned her separation from Justin. Various friends of Justin's spun her around the dance floor, but those dances served merely as interminable intermissions between dancing with Justin.

They spoke little. Cait surrendered to the music and the intoxicating feel of Justin holding her close, his hands warm against her back. Her feet seemed to float as she basked in the warmth of his body and relished the slow thud of his heart against her chest.

Only one incident marred the perfection of the evening. An older gentleman, a state senator, Cait thought, took her aside and told her his political party wanted Justin to get involved in politics. The man raved about the fact that, even for one so young, Justin was well respected in his section of the state, not to mention he had an impeccable reputation. The man added, with a wink, a wife like Cait didn't hurt, either. When Cait demurred, the man alluded, albeit with extreme delicacy, to her father's money and influence.

Cait quickly excused herself, but the specter of the yellow file raised its ugly head. Had Justin had her followed because he was concerned her activities might hurt his possible political future? He hadn't wanted to marry her. But he had. Because of her father's money? The sickening thought drained the blood from her head, and she clutched at the back of the nearest chair. No. She wouldn't, couldn't believe Justin was so venal.

She located him across the room. As if sensing her gaze, he looked her way. And smiled. A smile that complimented her and her red dress, and promised her he had plans for her later in the evening. Even as she felt the blush rising to her cheeks, Cait couldn't help grinning back. And not just because of the heated look in her husband's eye, which she couldn't see, but knew darned well was there. Justin didn't love her, but he did desire her. And he hadn't married her for her money or her father's business connections. He'd slept with Cait in her father's house, and his personal honor required that, as a consequence of his action, he marry her. Marriages the world over had succeeded on less. Especially when one of the two people involved was madly in love with the other.

Cait hugged one other thought close to her heart. Justin's last words as they entered the ballroom persuaded her he'd left her alone at night out of concern for her cat scratches. She'd ask him later.

Only she didn't. Later, she had other things on her mind. By the time Justin finally allowed her to fall asleep, she was barely capable of remembering her name. She did murmur his as she drifted off to dream he loved her.

"Come on, sleepyhead. Brunch at ten with your friends, remember?"

"Ten!" Cait tugged the covers over her head. "I'm sure I told you two."

Justin yanked the covers from her and lightly swatted her bare bottom. "Move it, lady. Your husband is starving."

She rolled onto her back and pulled up the covers. Justin was standing beside the bed knotting his tie. "Good morning." She smiled up at him.

"Good morning and quit smiling at me like that. Even if we had time, which we don't, you wore me out last night."

Cait stuck her tongue out at him and fled to the shower.

They descended in the elevator, Justin's arms wrapped around Cait. Her entire awareness centered on his mouth until the sound of a throat being cleared dragged her forcibly back to their surroundings. The elevator door stood open at the mezzanine.

"I don't know what it is about this elevator," Justin said gravely to the couple staring at them, "but the hotel ought to market it."

Cait managed to smile weakly at the man and woman as Justin swept her past them. "That was the same couple as last night," she hissed, her face hot with embarrassment.

"Yeah, poor guy. Right now he's wondering why the elevator doesn't affect his wife that way."

"His wife? What about him?"

"Ah, but the elevator doesn't affect me at all. The woman in the elevator with me, however..." Tanned skin crinkled at the corners of gray-green eyes.

A hand on her back guided Cait around an elegant, enormous Christmas tree. If her husband didn't stop giving her those slow, sexy smiles...

"Cait!"

At the sound of her name, Cait tore her gaze from her husband's face. The sight of the four people standing near the tall Christmas tree at the top of the escalator from the lobby brought a huge smile to her lips. Throwing wide her arms, she quickly moved to greet her friends, pulling Justin into the group. "Justin, I'd like you to meet Sarah and John Austen." She beamed at the black couple before hugging their ten-year-old. "And this is my slumber party buddy, Latisha." Then, reaching out with her free arm, Cait drew the carrot-topped woman closer. "This is Dorie Nicholson. Everybody, this is Justin."

Justin managed to herd the lively, talkative group past the tall fountain loaded with pale pink poinsettias and into the dining room, where they were quickly escorted to their table. The next minutes were taken up with the serious business of supplying themselves with food and drink.

Back from the buffet tables, Latisha immediately demanded to hear about Rascal and Nick. "Did they remember you?"

Cait slowly unfolded her white damask napkin. "I'm afraid Rascal died in an accident," she said gently. "Nick remembered me, and Justin has a new horse named Rosie, who's beautiful." Cait turned to Justin. "Latisha is crazy about horses."

"Cait and me, I mean, Cait and I read all the books in the library on horses," the girl solemnly told Justin. "Someday I'm going to ride one. Cait says you have lots of horses."

"Yes. Come down to the ranch and you can ride one."

Latisha sat up straight. "I wasn't hinting."

Justin didn't smile. "You'd be doing me a favor. When no one rides them, horses get fat and lazy."

The girl gave him a long look before turning to Cait. "You're right. He is nice."

"Latisha, eat your food before it gets cold," her mother scolded.

Cait reached over and squeezed Sarah's arm. "I'm so glad you could come. I've missed you. Especially your bossiness. Sarah treats me as if I'm her daughter's age," Cait said with a laugh to Justin.

Sarah shook her head. "Latisha already knows more about the real world than you did."

Cait made a face and looked across the table at Dorie. "Well?"

Every freckle on the woman's face lit up. "Yes."

Cait raised her champagne glass. "To Dorie." To Justin she explained, "Dorie passed her GED—General Educational Development test, so now she has a high school equivalency diploma. It's wonderful news, Dorie."

"Thanks to you." Dorie looked at Justin. "Cait insisted I do it, and she tutored me for ages. I would have quit months ago, but she wouldn't let me. I don't know what I would have done without her."

"You could have done it perfectly well on your own, and you know it," Cait said. "I'm the one who would have been lost if you and Sarah hadn't taken me under your wings. All the restaurants I've eaten in, you'd think I'd have known something about waiting tables."

"Waiting tables?" Justin asked.

"That's how I met Dorie and Sarah. At the restaurant. Most hostesses would have begged the manager to fire me after the first hour, but Sarah epitomizes patience." Immediately, everyone at the table chimed in with outrageous stories of Cait's first bungling days at the restaurant. Cait finally called them to order. "Enough about me and my ineptitude. Justin already thinks I'm a disaster waiting to happen." She related the details of her mishaps on the roof and with the bull.

Smiling, John shook his head. "Those things don't matter none, Cait. We like you even if you do have the dirtiest windows I've ever seen."

Cait laughed. "John works for a local manufacturer of windows. I swear, every time he came for dinner, he cleaned my windows. Talk about a busman's holiday."

"You fixed dinner?" Justin asked.

"Cait makes the world's best egg salad sandwiches," Latisha said loyally.

Cait gurgled with laughter. "That won't impress Justin. He hates egg salad."

Mirrors around the walls reflected back their laughing faces. Justin and John switched their interest to the Denver Broncos, and Cait smiled to see them deep in conversation. Outside the dining room, sunlight sparkled off a small lake. Inside, light streamed down from a domed, stained-glass skylight, picking out ornate carved moldings around the pale green and rose walls and ceiling. The sound of water bubbling from a fountain in the center of the room mingled with diners' voices, a baby's cry and the tinkle of dishes and silver, while muted strains of easy-listening music wafted in from the lower level. Pleased with the success of the brunch, Cait dipped her fork in the strawberry sauce covering her blintz.

When they pushed back their chairs and rose from the table, Cait felt stuffed and mellow. Exiting from the dining room, she dragged everyone over to some unoccupied chairs on the mezzanine and opened the large tote bag she'd brought along. "I know these aren't much—" she pulled out some gaily wrapped Christmas parcels "—but Merry Christmas." In answer to Latisha's eager inquiry, Cait urged everyone to open the packages. "I want to know what you think."

They were photographs. Cait had caught Sarah in the kitchen frosting a cake while John tried to steal a taste of icing and dodge the spatula aimed at his knuckles. Latisha sat at the table licking a beater and laughing. Love between the three burst from the photo. There was a portrait of a solemn Latisha daydreaming in a beam of light from a nearby window, and a picture of Latisha and Cait mugging for the camera in front of huge sandstone boulders in Garden of the Gods park. Cait had captured Dorie in a pensive mood as the woman studied.

"They are beautiful." Sarah spoke first. "Even if they weren't Cait Valentine originals, we'd treasure them always. Thank you."

Everyone echoed Sarah's sentiments, then pressed gifts on Cait. A cookbook and apron came from Sarah. Latisha shyly handed Cait a watercolor of a horse, which she admitted to Justin had been copied from one of Cait's photos of Rascal. John had framed the painting. Dorie gave Cait a calendar with Ansel Adams photographs.

Hugs and kisses and exclamations and thank-yous filled the air as Cait and Justin walked their guests to the car. The day was unseasonably mild for December, and only a slight breeze disturbed the huge red bows on the greenery-wrapped lampposts circling the hotel drive.

Cait waved until the Austens' car drove out of sight. "Thank you, Justin. I think everyone had a lovely time. I know I did."

"Did you, Cait? Which part did you enjoy the most? The one where I heard that for two years you've been waiting tables? Or maybe you got a laugh out of my hearing about your buying beat-up, used furniture in thrift shops and taking it home to paint so you'd have tables and chairs. My personal favorite was when your friends told about introducing you to consignment shops, where you could sell off your fancy party dresses so you'd have enough money to buy food. I'll bet you really enjoyed that part," he said savagely.

"Cait, darling. Is that you?" A tall, light-haired man hailed her from one of the shops on the hotel grounds. "I'm in a rush, but had to dash out and say hi. You must be the husband. I recognized you immediately." The man held out his hand to an annoyed and bewildered Justin. "Donald Clary," he said. "Cait shows in my gallery. Wonderful stuff. Wonderful. I'm glad she went back. That ranch stuff of hers is going to sell like hotcakes. I can feel it. Good meeting you. I have to run. Keep in touch, babe."

Justin turned to Cait, opened his mouth, shut it, did an abrupt about-face and strode back into the hotel.

Cait ran to keep up with him. "Justin."

"In our room," he snapped. "You've already made a fool of me in public once today."

In the elevator, he refused to even look at her.

CHAPTER SEVEN

THE extreme care Justin used to keep from slamming the door to their room told Cait more clearly than any words how angry he was. He had no right to be. "I don't know what you're so mad about. You knew what I've been doing."

His eyes glittered with fury as he faced her. "I certainly did not know my wife was waiting tables and selling her clothes so she could eat. How would I know? You sure didn't bother to mention it. I suppose the whole point of inviting your friends to brunch was to humiliate me in front of them."

"Humiliate you?"

He stood inches from her, his eyes hard as agates. "I want to know one thing," he ground out. "What the hell were you doing with your money?"

"Living on it."

"Damn it, Cait, you've been spending plenty of money," he said harshly. "If you weren't furnishing an apartment, buying clothes or food, what the hell were you spending it on?"

"I wasn't spending plenty of money. Waitresses don't make plenty of money."

Justin tore off his jacket and hurled it toward the bed. It fell to the floor. His tie followed. He unbuttoned his collar, rolled up his sleeves and shoved his fists into his trouser pockets. "I am talking about the money I sent you." Every coldly enunciated syllable rang as an insult.

Cait stared at him in stunned disbelief. "What money?"

"You know what money. The very generous allowance I sent you each month."

"You did not send me a generous allowance." She was so mad she could barely spit out the words.

"There speaks the daughter of Rafe Montgomery," he sneered. "Most women would think I'd been pretty damned generous. Especially considering you weren't doing a damned thing to deserve it. At least before, you earned it on your back."

"Of all the disgusting..." She snatched a pillow from the nearest bed and heaved it at him.

Justin didn't bother to duck. The pillow bounced off his stomach. "Maybe the last remark was uncalled for, but—"

"Uncalled for? You insult me and you lie and you accuse me of things I have no idea what you're talking about.... You're the one who hired someone to spy on me!"

"When you know you're wrong, you always start flinging outrageous accusations around."

"Oh, Justin, don't deny it." Shock and anger wore off to be replaced by a numbing depression. Moving to the window, Cait clutched at the sill and pressed her forehead against the cold glass. Clouds had moved in, blotting out the sunshine. The Canada geese huddled in clumps around the snow-rimmed lake looked as cold and miserable as she felt. "I saw the file," she said tonelessly, forcing herself to turn and face him.

"What file?"

"The one with the reports from the private detective you hired to follow me. I found it when I was sorting the papers in the ranch office. You removed it too late." In another mood she might have admired Justin's acting abilities. A person who didn't know better would have thought her husband had no clue what she was talking about. His expressions ran the gamut from bewildered to disbelieving to perturbed.

"Let me get this straight," Justin said slowly. "You found some kind of file in our office and something about it made you think I had a private detective following you?"

Cait blinked back angry tears. "Stop it, Justin. I read the reports. It was all there. Every move I made, every breath I took. Where I worked, who my friends were—you even had them investigated. How could you?" Stumbling to the upholstered chair in the corner, she crumpled into it.

"I don't know. I mean, I really didn't know." He looked mystified.

Cait wasn't fooled. "Last night when that senator or whoever he was said they wanted you in politics, I realized why you had me investigated. You were making sure I wasn't doing anything that would harm your political aspirations."

Justin stared at her for the longest time, but Cait had the impression he wasn't looking at her at all. Finally, she said tentatively, "Justin?"

He shook his head as if she'd awakened him. "I feel as if I've fallen down a rabbit hole. I don't know anything about any private detective, and I'm sure as hell not interested in running for political office. Are you sure about that file?" At her nod, he shook his head again. "Couldn't you have been confused about something else?"

"Justin, I am not blind or stupid. I read the reports. A private detective from this city has been following me since about a month after I moved here."

"I don't understand...." He frowned in thought. "A Colorado Springs detective. Do you remember his name?"

"Of course not," she said impatiently. "How would I remember—no, wait. I remember thinking the name sounded too appropriate for a detective to be true. Let me think...." She shut her eyes and tried to picture the letterhead in her mind. "W. E. Trace. Yes, that was it."

She'd barely uttered the name before Justin was thumbing through the phone book. "Here it is. W. E. Trace, Investigations." He dialed the number, listened a few minutes, then hung up. "Just a recording. He probably wouldn't tell us anything anyway. Such as who hired him."

"Does this mean you believe me about the file?"

"Yes. If you say you saw it, you did."

Cait produced a wobbly smile. "Thank you."

"And?" Justin prompted.

He wanted to know if she believed him. She did, but one thing troubled her. "I believe you didn't hire the private detective to follow me, but if you didn't, who did? And who removed the file?" Her breath caught at a new idea. "Do you think the detective broke in and stole the reports back?"

"I can't imagine why." He shoved a matching chair to a spot in front of her and, sitting, eyed her thoughtfully. "Why didn't you come to me with the file when you found it?"

"I was going to, but then the file was gone, and I assumed you took it. I mean, who else would have?"

"Are you sure whatever you saw isn't still there? That office was really in a mess. Could the file have been mislaid?"

"By whom?"

"Good question. Did you tell anyone else about the file?"

"No."

Justin stood up and started to pace. "Someone must have seen it or known about it...." He came to a halt. "Harry."

"I know she doesn't like me, but I can't see her hiring a private eye," Cait objected.

"Cait," Justin said with exaggerated patience, "the file was in the ranch office. Two people use that office on a regular basis. One of us didn't know about the file. The other has been in a nursing home and couldn't have removed it."

She thought about that a minute. "But Hank could call Mrs. Courtney and ask her to get it," she guessed.

"Exactly."

She should have known there was more to Hank's insisting she return to the ranch. There must be something in the file that he thought would persuade Justin to divorce her.

"We'll tackle Hank tomorrow about what the hell he was thinking, but for now—" Justin walked back and leaned over her chair, resting his hands on the padded arms "—let's get back to the money. I promise I won't lose my temper, but I would like to know where all that money I sent you every month went."

Cait's body turned to stone. Any sense of restored calm immediately disintegrated. "Why do you keep saying that?" Her fingernails gouged into her palms. "You know you never mailed me a dime. When I first left, I sent you a note telling you what hotel I was at. You didn't call. You didn't write. Later, when I knew you weren't..." Pushing the pain back to its hiding place, she swallowed hard. "Later, when I moved to an apartment, I sent you that address. You never bothered to write back."

Justin straightened and stalked over to the window. "What was I supposed to write, Cait? Tell you to get the hell back to the ranch?'' He flung the words over his shoulder. "Maybe you thought I'd chase you down and haul you back. So you could leave me again the next time your nose was out of joint or things didn't quite go the way you wanted." His back to her, he shook his head. "I had no intention of playing that kind of game." He turned and rested his hip on the windowsill. "Now, about that money," he began in an implacable voice. "Where is it?"

His closed face told her she'd been tried and convicted. She hardly knew what the crime was. Her body sagged in the chair. "Where do you think? That I spent it on boyfriends? That I lost it in the stock market? That I blew it at the dog track?" He looked at her. Waiting. After a moment, she hauled herself out of the chair and went over to her purse. Taking out her checkbook, she threw it at him.

He made no effort to catch it. "I've seen the bank statements."

His admission stunned her. Anger, furious, overwhelming and red-hot, erupted as the full impact of his deception slammed into her. "You dirty, rotten liar." Cait flung her purse at him. His catching it with one hand further infuriated her. "You did have a private eye checking on me." She dashed angry tears from her face. "I should have known it wasn't Hank."

"What the hell are you talking about now?"

"You admitted you've been snooping, reading my bank statements."

"Damn it, Cait, you never balanced a checkbook in your life. After I started the account for you, I had the statements sent to me to be sure you didn't run short of money. The way you were bleeding that ATM, I—"

She lifted her head. "What did you say?"

"I said I had the statements sent to me—"

"Not that. You said automatic teller machine. What bank?" At the look on his face, she insisted, "Humor me."

He named the bank in a long-suffering voice.

Cait quickly crossed the room, picked up her checkbook and thrust it at him. "Look at it. Different bank. And Sarah made me cut up my ATM card a couple of months after I started work. She said it was too big a temptation." Digging her wallet out of her purse, she handed it to him. "Look. You won't find an ATM card." Her watch showed the time. "Sarah should be home by now. Call her. She knows where I bank. So does Dorie."

Justin thumbed through her checkbook. Then he went through it a second time, more slowly. Deep furrows etched his forehead. "I opened an account for you," he said deliberately. "I sent you your ATM card, your personal identification number and the checkbook. I deposited the money by mail. I have your bank statements and mine to prove it."

"And I can't prove anything, so I'm the liar, is that it?" Without waiting for an answer, Cait dashed across the room and hauled her suitcase from the closet, slinging it onto the bed. Jerking her clothes from hangers, she threw them into the open suitcase.

Justin didn't move. "Going somewhere?"

Grabbing her clothes from a drawer, without looking at the item in her hand, she wadded it up and fired it at him. "Yes!" She disappeared into the bathroom to gather up her toiletries.

When she came out, Justin was lying on his back on the other bed, his hands up in the air swinging a red scrap of lace-edged silk. Embarrassment brought Cait to a screeching halt, but she quickly recovered. Fine. He could have a souvenir. She ignored him as he inserted a hand in each leg and slid the underwear down his arms.

When he began swinging it around his forefinger, in what he obviously intended to be a very provocative and annoying gesture, she paid no attention. Just because the lingerie was part of a matched set...just because it had cost her an arm and a leg...just because she'd bought it special before returning to the ranch...

Whirling around, she reached out to snatch back her underwear. The next instant, she was flat on her back on the bed, Justin sprawled on top of her. He stretched her arms above her head on the pillow and wrapped the red silk around her wrists. "Get off me," she grated through clenched teeth. She refused to sink to his level and struggle.

Instead of releasing her, he scrutinized every inch of her face and then said in a contemplative voice, "You're wrong about your nose. I think it's perfect for your face."

"I don't give a damn what you think about anything." If she didn't yell at him, she'd bawl.

Justin gave her a reproving look. "When did you start swearing? I'll bet your mother would have washed your mouth out with soap for using language like that."

Cait opened her mouth to assure him her mother most definitely would not have. Justin slid his tongue between her lips. And gave a whole new meaning to washing out one's mouth. She was trembling when he finally lifted his head.

"When you first came back, I warned you," he said softly. "I can be every bit as stubborn and strong-willed as you are."

"Flexing your muscles doesn't impress me," Cait snapped, hiding behind anger. "That macho junk died with the buffalo herds."

Heavy dark eyebrows registered mocking skepticism. "I could have sworn it excited you."

"It repulsed me."

His eyes danced with laughter. "I could tell by the way you kissed me."

Cait went rigid. His making fun of her was absolutely the last straw. "I'm going to kill you."

"Do it later, Cait. I've got something else in mind right now." He lowered his head.

Anger couldn't protect her from his kisses. "No. Justin, please. Don't." She turned her head away. "You can't want to make love to a woman you think is a liar and a thief." A tear rolled from the corner of her eye across her cheek toward her ear.

Justin caught the tear with the tip of his tongue. "I don't." He gently nipped her earlobe with his teeth.

She squeezed her eyes tightly to hold back a second tear. "And I don't want to make love to a man who thinks I'm a liar and a thief—" the tear slipped out "—but if you start kissing me, I won't be able to say no."

"Truthful Cait." Justin brushed away her tear with his lips. "You might refuse to answer or give evasive answers, but you don't lie. I don't understand what happened to the money, but I believe you don't know anything about it." He trailed soft kisses down the side of her neck.

Cait rolled her head so she could see Justin's face. "But you said—"

"I said I can prove I deposited the money. You wouldn't think a man would forget how quick a certain woman fires up, would you? I didn't go off half-cocked when you said you could prove you hadn't spent it."

"It sounded like an accusation," she said defensively.

Justin dropped a kiss on her nose. "I was thinking out loud," he said. "Look at the facts. One, I put the money in the bank. Two, you didn't take it out. Three, someone did."

She caught her breath in dismay. "I hadn't thought that far." She saw his mouth quiver and said, "Don't you dare say I never think things out."

"I wouldn't dream of it," he said in a solemn voice.

"Yes, you would," she said halfheartedly, her mind on something else. "We need to start investigating to find out who's been stealing your money."

"Where do you plan to start?"

"The bank, of course," she said impatiently, trying to shift him off her with her hips.

"Even if it wasn't Sunday afternoon and the bank closed, what do you think they could tell us? They have no way of knowing who's been using your ATM card. The only thing we can do is close out the account first thing in the morning. And maybe see if that detective Hank hired can find out anything, like if anyone in your apartment building came unexpectedly into money during the past two years. In the meantime—" he gave her a warm, lazy smile "—I'm on a bed with a woman who's obviously turned on by having her hands tied over her head with red silk—"

"I am not." She wasn't lying. The turn-on was the sexy smile slowly curving his lips, his masculine scent, their mingled heartbeats, the slumberous look in his eyes. She was fairly certain sleep wasn't what was on his mind.

"Too bad, because all that squirming you're doing is having a definite effect on me."

Having her hands tied together didn't inhibit Cait in the least.

Afterward, she lay beneath the tousled sheet, her leg touching Justin's leg from hip to ankle, her heart gradually returning to its normal steady beat. The crinkly hairs on his leg rasped against her sensitized skin, contributing to her mellow, satisfied mood. Cait's hand rested on his warm hipbone.

Fighting the temptation to allow fingers to stray, she forced her thoughts down other pathways. Justin's conclusion that Hank, for some unknown reason, had hired the private detective was probably right, but even if Hank didn't want Justin sending money to Cait, he wouldn't have stolen the money. So who had? "Justin," Cait said drowsily, "what if you never find out who stole your money?"

He didn't answer. Cait smiled in the fading light and complacently wiggled her toes. Between last night and this afternoon, Justin must have worn himself out. She wouldn't disturb him. There would be pleasure enough in watching him sleep. Moving carefully, she elevated her upper body and propped her head on her hand. The smile on her face faded.

His tanned skin contrasting sharply with the white bed linen, Justin lay awake. The brooding look on his stone-carved face spelled trouble.

In spite of the heat his body gave off, Cait felt chilled clear through. "Justin?" Hesitantly she brushed her fingers across his tightened lips. "Is something the matter?"

"Hell no, Cait. Everything's just dandy. Why would you even ask?"

Her stomach heaved at the cold, clipped words, and she eyed him warily. "You have a funny look on your face."

"A funny look. I don't know why that would be," he said in a meditative voice. "I sure as hell can't think of much funny right now. My wife ran off and left me, my uncle hired a private eye to follow her, and somebody's been robbing me for two years. But do you know what's the least funny of all, Cait?"

"No." She barely breathed the one-word answer.

"That my wife thinks I'm a sleazy, no-account husband who would allow two years to pass without once wondering how she was eating, how she was living, what she was using for money."

"You sent me money. It wasn't your fault I didn't receive it."

"You didn't know I thought I was providing for you. As far as you knew, I didn't give a damn how my wife was supporting herself." The eyes staring at the ceiling held all the warmth and color of a frozen lake.

"Justin, no, you have it all wrong."

"What's wrong, Cait, is us. We never should have married."

"Pay attention to your discards, Cait. I swear, if I played with Nick, I'd get a better game," Hank groused. "Gin."

Cait glanced down at the dog lying by her feet and shifted the cat in her lap before gathering up and shuffling the playing cards. "What difference does my paying attention make? You still win."

Hank gave her a sharp look. "You and Justin were both lying to me on the phone, weren't you?"

"I don't know what you're talking about." She carefully dealt out their hands.

"I'm talking about how, when I was in the nursing home, neither one of you mentioned the way you can barely stand being in the same room with the other. I'm talking about how I never had a notion you were sleeping in different bedrooms. I'm talking about how you're counting the days until Christmas and your anniversary so you can run away again."

"You know what they say—" Cait concentrated on sorting her cards "—a person's gotta do what a person does best. Running away's what I do best." If only she'd run away before their marriage so Justin wasn't spending his days—and nights—cursing the day they'd met. She slammed the door on that thought. Mourning the death of a marriage that had never lived was best done late at night with only a damp pillowcase as witness. "You must be about to choke on all those I-told-you-sos you're swallowing."

"Come off it, Cait. I know how you toughed things out the past two years. I'm the one who hired a detective to keep tabs on you, remember?"

"It's hard to forget being spied on," she retorted.

"Hard to forget or hard to forgive? I told you I got to feeling guilty, like maybe I'd been too hard on you and drove you off. When you didn't run home to your dad, I got worried. I hired Trace to keep an eye on you, make sure you were okay. Are you so mad at me you're willing to break up your marriage just to spite me?"

"Giving you and Justin your hearts' desire hardly seems like spite." Cait forced a lighthearted note into her voice.

"Who said it's my heart's desire?" Hank asked gruffly. "Maybe I've gotten used to you."

"And maybe cows will fly over the moon." She wasn't married to Hank. It was his nephew who regretted her existence. "Your play."

He selected a card. "How come you didn't tell Justin about our little deal?"

"I'm waiting for the right time. And—" she forestalled his next question "—I might not be much of a cardplayer, but I'm the best you got, so if you want me to keep playing, you'll mind your own business."

"Justin is my business. All right, all right," he said hastily as Cait picked up Lucy and started to stand. "Don't work yourself into a tizzy." He tossed down a discard. "What do you want me to talk about?"

"You could start with thanking me for putting up the outside Christmas lights."

Hank peered from under sun-bleached eyebrows. "Way I heard it, Justin and Lane ended up putting them up."

"A mere technicality. It was my idea."

"I suppose this fool Christmas tree," he said, nodding toward the corner, "was your idea, too."

"Yes, and I like it and Marie likes it, so watch what you say."

"What do you know about Marie?"

"She lived with you so I know she was a saint."

"Who's a saint?" Marilee breezed into the living room, a whiff of outdoor air clinging to her.

"Cait thinks Marie was, to live with an old goat like me."

"Nonsense, Uncle Hank, you're a big teddy bear." Marilee moved across the room and kissed his cheek. "Not that I don't think Marie was a wonderful woman," she added quickly. "A person can tell by her picture how special she was." She went over to the fireplace and studied the photographs on the mantel. "You'll laugh, but I feel like her spirit is still on the place."

"So do I," said Cait, surprised to discover she and Marilee would have this, of all things, in common.

A scornful glance bounced off Cait before Marilee turned to Hank. "Have you ever wondered what your daughter would have been like if she'd lived? I'll bet she'd love to cook and sew and keep house. All the men in the area would be courting her."

Cait ran her fingers lightly over Lucy's soft fur. Marilee was as subtle as a ten-ton truck.

Hank leaned back in his chair. "It's funny you should bring up little Mary Amanda. Lying around waiting for this darned hip to mend, I had plenty of time to think about her. I figured Mary Amanda would have been a carbon copy of Marie, but the more I thought on it... Marie and me, we waited so long for that little girl, we'd have spoiled her rotten. She'd probably have been wild as a March hare, half horse, crazy about animals, and she would have worshiped the ground Justin walks on."

"Interesting." Marilee gave Cait a bitter smile. "He just described you. You sure know how to play your cards right."

"Hank wasn't describing me." Cait found Marilee's conclusions more disconcerting than the nasty tone Marilee had voiced them in. "Just because I like animals... I mean, I certainly don't worship the ground Justin walks on."

"No one would argue with that statement."

The cold words froze Cait's spine. "Justin," she said weakly, turning slightly, "I didn't hear you come in."

He met that inanity with a scathing look before turning his attention to his cousin's wife. "Marilee, these two cardsharps are obviously too involved in their cutthroat dealings to remember their manners. Why don't you take off your coat and stay awhile? What's that you're carrying?"

Marilee looked blankly at the large, foil-covered china dish in her hands. "This? Oh." Her smile didn't quite make it to her eyes. "I got up extra early this morning and cooked up a nice batch of tapioca pudding for Uncle Hank. I know Harry's too busy to bother about special food for our invalid."

"I'm not an invalid," Hank said testily, "and Harry's cooking is just fine."

"You're so loyal, Uncle Hank. You stick up for everyone. I'll take this to the kitchen and bring you back a bowl of pudding."

"Don't go to any bother. I'll eat it later."

"You can't get well if you don't eat right," Marilee scolded. "Tapioca pudding is good for you."

"Thanks, Marilee, I'm not hungry right now."

"You don't fool me." Marilee playfully shook her finger at Hank. "I know you think you hate tapioca pudding, but as soon as you taste mine, you'll change your mind. I'm going to fix you a bowlful this minute and stand over you while you eat it."

Justin crossed his arms and leaned against the wall. "Maybe it will sweeten you up."

Hank threw Cait a desperate look. Cait set the kitten on the floor and stepped over Nick. "I know how busy you are, Marilee. I'll fix Hank's bowl of pudding."

Marilee held the dish out of Cait's reach. "Don't touch this food. You've been petting that filthy cat."

"Don't be silly. Lucy cleans herself a hundred times a day." Cait grabbed the dish and headed into the hall toward the kitchen.

Busy evading Marilee's determined hands, Cait failed to see the kitten now grooming herself in the middle of the hallway. Cait's booted foot came down on Lucy's tail, and the kitten let out an earsplitting howl. Cait leaped backward, crashed into the coatrack, spun around to dodge the toppling rack with its flailing coats and somehow managed to hook her heel on the bottom step of the hall staircase. Teetering wildly for what seemed an eternity, she fought for balance, but lost the battle, falling heavily.

Her body ended up sprawled across the bottom of the staircase. "Oh, no!" Appalled, Cait stared at the puddle of creamy tapioca pudding on the floor at the base of the stairs. Shards of china stuck up from the mess like spines on a porcupine. "Marilee, I'm so sorry. After all your work."

Marilee raised stunned eyes from the spreading pool. Her face contorted with anger. "You did that on purpose. You deliberately threw my pudding on the floor."

"It was an accident. I didn't see Lucy—"

"Save your lies for feeble old men," Marilee hissed. "You can't fool me."

Justin came on the run. "Are you all right?" he asked in a clipped voice.

"A little shaken is all," Cait said.

Justin stepped around the mess on the floor and helped her up. He caught the wince she tried to conceal and asked, "Sure you're okay?"

Hank appeared in the living room doorway, leaning over his walker, and echoed Justin's question.

"Certainly she's okay," Marilee snapped. "She goes from one stupid disaster to another and all you men fall all over yourselves rescuing her instead of seeing she's just a spoiled brat who'll do anything to be the center of attention."

"I'll buy you a new dish, of course," Cait said stiffly.

"I don't want a dish or anything else from you. You might be able to buy your way into or out of everything else but you can't buy me or Lane." Marilee slammed out the front door.

Hank spoke into the awkward silence. "Marilee's sure had a burr under her saddle lately."

Justin studied Cait through narrowed eyes. "Your entire backside will probably be black and blue by tomorrow."

The unsympathetic voice and heartless words stung. "I'll be fine," Cait said, blinking rapidly. She gave Mrs. Courtney an apologetic smile as the housekeeper came from the kitchen with bucket and rags. "I'm sorry about the mess."

Justin commandeered the cleaning supplies and handed them to Cait. "Was Marilee right? Did you drop it on purpose?"

"What if she did?" Hank growled. "Marilee can be a real pain in the neck."

Mrs. Courtney nodded. "I've been tempted more than I like to say to throw Little Miss Homemaker with her interfering ways out of my kitchen, but I've never had the nerve to do it. I'm not saying Cait did it on purpose," she added hastily.

The unexpected support from Hank and Mrs. Courtney failed to lift Cait's spirits. Or sidetrack her anger over Justin's unfair insinuations. It wasn't Cait's fault she hadn't seen Lucy.

Justin surveyed the three of them grimly. "Cait's bad enough. She doesn't need you two encouraging her. If you're going to take sides, you ought to be on Marilee's side. In case you've forgotten, Marilee's dad abandoned his family shortly after Marilee's birth, and her mom's made a lifetime career of shacking up with one cattle tramp after another. Maybe Marilee does get kind of pushy at times, but that's because she's trying too hard. She wants desperately to belong." He looked at Cait. "You might try showing a little compassion the next time you're tempted to toss her efforts on the ground."

"Now, Justin," Hank said, "it could have been an accident."

Ruthlessly suppressing her hurt and anger, Cait sat back on her heels, the messy rag in her hand, and looked squarely up at Justin, her head bent back until her neck ached. His gray-green eyes reminded her of hoarfrost. "All right. I admit it. It wasn't an accident. Marilee irritated me, so I deliberately threw the pudding on the floor and broke her dish."

CHAPTER EIGHT

JUSTIN laughed.

Hank snorted. "Well, if you didn't, you should have. She'd have crammed that damned stuff down my throat...." Grumbling, he hobbled back into the living room, his walker clumping against the wooden floor.

Mrs. Courtney returned to the kitchen with the cleaning supplies.

Ignoring the hand Justin held out to her, Cait scrambled to her feet and stared stonily at him, hopefully hiding the fact that his laughter completely bewildered her. Silently she dared him to attack her further, knowing if he said one more word of censure, she'd dissolve into tears.

Still smiling, Justin brushed aside a lock of hair that had flopped down over her eye. "Sure you're all right?"

Fighting the insidious temptation to curl into the palm resting warmly against her cheek, she held herself rigid. "I'm fine. I faked the fall after I threw the pudding on the floor, so naturally I was careful about how I fell."

"You have more trouble lying than anyone I know."

"Add it to the long list you keep of my failings," she said flippantly.

"I don't blame you for being mad," he began.

"How charitable of you not to blame me for something. And here I thought I was the root of all evil, to blame for war, world poverty, starvation and the common cold." Angry tears clogged the back of her throat.

"I'm trying to apologize, but you're not making it easy."

Cait drew an imaginary mark in the air. "Chalk up another crime for Cait."

"I'm damned if I'll grovel." Justin yanked her up against his hard body, covering her mouth with a large, callused hand. "Be quiet and listen. I saw you lying on the staircase and I went a little haywire. I know you're perfectly capable of disposing of Marilee's pudding in such a harebrained way to rescue Hank from what he believes is a fate worse than death, and all I could think of was what a damned stupid thing to do, risking an injury over something as stupid as tapioca pudding. I wanted to wring—" His face darkened. "Damn it, now what?"

In spite of her best efforts, tears spilled from Cait's overflowing eyes. Furious at her weakness, she babbled incoherently against his palm.

"What? Are you in pain?" Justin removed his hand. "Do you think you broke something?"

Cait took a deep breath and regained a semblance of control. "Yes, I broke something. I deliberately broke Marilee's dish, and I'm deliberately going to break your head."

"You didn't deliberately break anything," Justin said in a disgusted voice, "which I should have realized immediately, because you'd never do anything that harmed or endangered an animal. The way Lucy caterwauled, I gather she tripped you up. I apologize for jumping all over you."

"I don't want your stupid apology. I want you to let go of me so I can check on Lucy."

Justin's arm tightened around her waist. "The cat's fine. She came streaking into the living room, bent on taking refuge behind the bookcase, but I managed to catch her and check her out. The only damage was to her dignity. Plus she's spitting mad. She must get her temper from you." He rubbed moisture from Cait's cheek with his thumb. "You're going to make me grovel, aren't you?"

"Give me one reason why I shouldn't." Cait had to do something with her hands so she raised them to Justin's chest and traced the soft plaid lines of his flannel shirt. She must not have sounded very hard-hearted because he laughed softly and tugged her face upward until her eyes met his. As if she could be swayed by rueful gray-green eyes. Dropping her gaze, she focused on Justin's strong, tanned jaw. "I think groveling would be good for you."

"I'll grovel all you want if you tell me just one thing. Am I wrong in thinking you are perfectly capable of dumping Marilee's pudding on the floor?"

"You are very definitely wrong. I never, ever would," she said emphatically. "You are wrong, wrong, wrong."

"Then I owe you a double apology."

"Yes, you do." Before she could savor her vindication, a small giggle escaped, betraying her.

Justin wrapped a hand around the back of her head and lowered his face until their noses were inches apart. "Why don't you share the joke?"

She assumed an innocent expression. "Marilee's right about one thing. She makes the best tapioca pudding I've ever eaten, and I'm crazy about tapioca pudding."

Justin grasped the point immediately. "You weren't taking the pudding to the kitchen to rescue Hank. You were going to eat it."

Gray-green eyes brimming with laughter ought to be registered as deadly weapons. Several hours later, Cait still held that opinion. Along with the conviction that those same laughing eyes had absolutely, positively, bewitched her from the first instant she'd encountered them. Cait removed Lucy from the open drawer the kitten was investigating. In all fairness, it wasn't only Justin's eyes; it was his smile that reduced her to a mindless automaton worshiping at his booted feet.

Only that wasn't true, either. Stepping over a sprawling Nick, she carried a folded pile of clothing into Justin's bedroom. The kitten gamboled along at her side. Cait was intimately acquainted with Justin's faults. He wasn't always the most patient of men, and he gave short shrift to hands who shirked their duties, mistreated animals, lied or cheated. He expected a lot, sometimes too much, of other people, and had little use for whiners and immature, tantrum throwers.

The drawer in the tall chest was empty. A lonely pair of her underwear rested in a second drawer. They must have been in the laundry hamper the day she'd left two years ago. Slowly, Cait opened a third drawer. The empty, yawning space sent her straight to the closet. Justin had used the right side of the huge closet. Having avoided the closet since her return, Cait stared in astonishment at the closet bar on the left that held nothing more than bare hangers. The closet and her drawers were as she'd left them two years ago. Justin had anticipated her return.

Cait stumbled to the bed and sat on the edge, her initial burst of euphoria vanishing. Empty drawers had nothing to do with love. Empty drawers, like money regularly deposited in a bank account, demonstrated Justin's commitment to his marriage vows. His repurchasing Rosie made sense now. In spite of a little thing like a runaway wife, Justin continued to fulfill his responsibilities and carry out his side of the marital bargain. Love would have sent him chasing after Cait to drag her back. Duty compelled him to send money, leave space in the closet, even replace a horse, in case his wife returned.

The discovery ought to cause jubilation because it proved Justin would let her stay. As long as she wanted. Lucy leaped up to land in Cait's lap, and Cait automatically stroked the soft fur of the small stray. Justin's teasing words that Cait and the kitten were alike held more truth than he knew. Lots of strays found refuge on the ranch.

With a sigh, Cait set down the cat and went for another load of clothing. From below came the rumble of Lane's voice at the front door. Lane was another stray. His parents had divorced when Lane was seven, and his father, Wylie, had given his son little besides the Rutherford name and looks. Hank said Wylie traveled through life ignoring the damage he left in his wake. Hank had added that one could never trust Wylie because he was totally selfish, and in Wylie's priorities, Wylie always came first.

Cait dumped her socks in the drawer. Lane's mother, Doreen, had remarried when Lane was eighteen. Cullen Norris was nice, but he had no interest in his wife's son. Having met Doreen, Cait was well aware Lane's mother ignored the fact that Hank had paid good money for Wylie's share of the ranch. As far as Doreen was concerned, Hank was merely holding Wylie's share in trust for Lane. Eight years ago when Lane was twenty-four, Doreen had persuaded Hank to take Lane on as a ranch hand. Four years later, Lane had married Marilee, and the two had moved into the old ranch house. Sometimes Cait felt Lane shared Doreen's opinion that Wylie's share somehow belonged to Lane.

Two months ago, Cait would have sworn their opinion was not shared by Hank. Hank owned two-thirds of the ranch, but Justin had won the position of foreman at age twenty-two after he'd graduated from Colorado State University. There was no doubt in anyone's mind that Justin now ran the place. While Lane was more than a regular hand, he was less than a foreman, and Hank had never indicated he was grooming Lane for part ownership in the ranch. Until he'd made his crazy threat in the hospital.

Maybe Hank, like Justin, felt sorry for Lane. Justin blamed much of his cousin's behavior on Lane's fatherless upbringing. Ranching was a way of life, a religion for Justin. Cait had no proof, but she'd always thought Lane took after his dad more than Justin and Hank realized. She stopped in the middle of the hall, her arms draped with clothes on hangers. A psychologist would undoubtedly accuse her of being jealous of Lane. She wasn't. Even if Justin was more forgiving of Lane's transgressions than of Cait's.

Or maybe it had simply seemed that way. Thoughtfully she hung up her clothing. The year she'd lived here, her behavior toward Lane and Marilee certainly merited no good-conduct medals. It was time she accepted that Justin had family besides her. Christmas was as good a time to start as any.

"You want to have Christmas dinner here and you're going to do the cooking?" Justin asked that night, standing in the middle of his bedroom after Cait announced her intentions.

He couldn't have loaded his voice with more skepticism if he'd tried. Cait gave him a confident smile. "It's impossible to be a waitress for almost two years without learning something about cooking." Feigning a casual air, she strolled to the other side of the bed and extracted her pajamas from under the pillow. "Mrs. Courtney told Hank she and Court would like to spend Christmas with her sister and family in Denver. Hank said we could eat out or heat something in the microwave, but that's not right, not on Christmas.'' She could barely hear herself speak above the pounding of her heart. ''Sarah gave me cooking lessons, so don't worry, you won't starve to death.''

She started to unbutton her shirt, then, losing her nerve, she bolted to the bathroom, snapping the lock behind her. She collapsed on the side of the tub, the porcelain chilling her skin through her jeans. In Justin's absence, making the decision to move into the master bedroom required no courage. Carrying out the decision under his contemplative gaze was something else entirely.

She must be absolutely insane. Just because he hadn't tossed Lucy from the bed the night she'd joined them... Just because he'd smiled at her today, the first time since they'd come back from Colorado Springs... Just because Cait hated sleeping alone across the hall... Her fingers closed around the horseshoe charm at the base of her throat. Knuckles rapping sharply on the door startled her. ''What?''

''You sleeping in the tub tonight?''

The amusement in his voice put steel in her spine. And gave her hope. Justin wouldn't be laughing at her if he intended to kick her out of his bed. ''I'm brushing my teeth,'' she lied.

''Hell,'' he snorted, ''if they're as yellow as the rest of you, it'll take you forever. I'll use the other bathroom.''

That was fine with her. Especially if he was going to call her a coward. She wasn't a coward. At least, not a big coward. Maybe a little coward.

When Cait finally emerged from the bathroom, Justin had beaten her into bed. He watched her as she puttered with her things, putting off the moment when she crawled in beside him. Not that her intentions could be any secret to him as he lay there, his hands folded beneath his head, the covers pulled up to his waist. Light from the overhead fixture bounced off wide shoulders and muscled arms. His broad chest, with its fading summer tan, rose and fell rhythmically. And not nearly as fast as her beating heart.

He cocked a heavy eyebrow. "Do you plan to stay up all night fidgeting around the bedroom?"

She figured her options were to slug him or to climb into bed. Despite the appeal of wiping the amused arrogance off his face, climbing into bed was probably safer. "I'm not fidgeting." She snapped off the overhead light and walked to the side of the bed, glaring at him across the wide expanse of sheets. "A woman can't get a decent night's sleep on that other mattress, either, so I'm sleeping in here from now on." Turning off the lamp beside the bed, she flopped down on the mattress and yanked the covers up to her chin.

"Is that so?" Justin asked mildly.

"And what's more," she added, bravery coming more easily in the dark, "you were pretty outspoken about my not earning my keep in the bedroom, so—"

"I apologize for that remark."

"You can keep your stupid apology." Rolling over onto her side, she raised herself up on one elbow. Enough moonlight filtered into the room to let her see the guarded expression on his face. She scowled at him. "I've been exhausting myself decorating for Christmas, entertaining your uncle, sorting the mess in your office and lots more. What have you done besides play with cows? Maybe it's time you earned your keep on your back."

Stark silence met her outrageous pronouncement. Then Justin laughed and drew her head downward. "Never let it be said," he muttered against her mouth, "that Justin Valentine shirks his duty."

Much, much later, lying warmly at Justin's side, Cait thought he certainly hadn't shirked anything tonight. His response prompted her to voice the question she wouldn't have the courage to ask in the light of day. "Justin, this, at night, has always been good between us. When I came back, I wanted to, that is, I was willing..." She inhaled deeply and tried again. "Why did you tell me to sleep in the other room?"

"I didn't." His thumb circled lazily around her hipbone.

Cait stiffened indignantly. "Yes, you did. The first morning. You told me I had plenty of time to move my things into the spare bedroom."

"You did." He trailed his fingers across her stomach. "You had plenty of time to not move them, too. You made the choice."

"You're telling me you didn't care?"

"What I'm telling you, Cait," he said evenly, "is you made the choice to marry me and come out here, and you made the choice to leave. If you don't want to be married to me, don't want to sleep with me, I'm not about to beg or force you into my bed. Marriage is two people walking side by side, not one constantly chasing after the other to haul her back. When we first got married, you blamed me every blasted time something didn't go your way. Life doesn't work that way. You have to take responsibility for your actions. To me, marriage means a lifetime of commitment. What it means to you..." He paused. "After Christmas, going or staying, only you can make that choice."

In other words, he didn't give a big fat darn if she left or stayed. That was going to change. As soon as he learned what Cait had done for him, making a bargain with Hank to save the ranch for Justin, then her husband would give a darn. He'd gratefully beg her to stay. Rolling away from Justin, she curled into a tight little ball. Sleeping with someone could be lonelier than sleeping alone.

Lane and Marilee blew in through the office door, Lane fighting the wind to shut the door behind them. "Where's everyone?" Lane asked. "Justin said yesterday he wanted to see us this afternoon. A family meeting."

"Hank and Justin were in the kitchen having coffee the last I saw them," Cait said. The couple went through the office into the main part of the house. Cait turned back to the computer screen, trying to ignore the deep hurt caused by Lane's words. Justin had said nothing to her about a family meeting. She punched in more calving data. Lane had said "us" meaning Marilee's presence had been requested, but obviously no one considered Cait a member of the family. Not that she cared the least little bit. Struggling to convince herself of that point, she didn't hear Justin enter the office.

"Come into the living room," he said abruptly. Without waiting for a response, he wheeled and walked away.

Cait lifted suddenly clumsy fingers from the keyboard. The shuttered look on Justin's face was the one he wore when forced to perform a repugnant chore such as destroying an ill or injured animal or firing an unsatisfactory ranch hand. She grabbed at the desk, her fingernails digging into the wood. He was going to tell her to leave, that he wanted a divorce. Slowly she pushed back her chair. No. Justin wouldn't humiliate her by ordering her off the ranch in front of his family. Nor would he go back on his promise to let her stay until after Christmas. He'd told her the choice was hers. He wouldn't change his mind. But whatever the situation waiting in the living room, she doubted it would be pleasant.

Justin turned to Marilee the minute Cait appeared. "I want the file you stole returned immediately." He forestalled her protest. "Don't bother denying it. You gave yourself away when you tried to embarrass Cait about her friends at a time when you couldn't possibly have known who her friends were. Unless you'd read the file. I don't know how you knew about it—"

"She came into the office when I was reading it," Cait belatedly recalled.

Justin kept his attention on Marilee. "I assume you took it that night when you and Lane came over to use the hot tub."

Marilee shrugged. "Cait was obviously angry about what was in the file, so I was curious."

"And when you saw what it was, you took it because you needed to know if the private detective had figured out you'd been stealing the money I'd deposited in the bank for Cait."

Cait heard her own breathing in the tense silence following Justin's harsh accusation. Marilee might have stolen the file, but the money? Cait didn't believe it, and she said so.

"Believe it, Cait," Justin said heavily. "She was going to town, and I asked her to mail some stuff. The envelope with your bank card felt overweight, so I told her what it was and that it was important to make sure there was enough postage on it. I also gave her a package of blank checks to mail to you."

Marilee's face blanched. She started to say something, then looked down at her hands knotted in her lap. The silence dragged on. Finally, Marilee said in a small voice, "Cait's dad is loaded. If she needed money, she could have asked him."

"That's hardly the point, Marilee," Justin said. "It wasn't your money, but you used the ATM card to withdraw funds every time you went up to Colorado Springs."

Marilee's shocking admission of guilt took Cait totally by surprise. Glancing over at Hank, Cait saw the deep, devastating disappointment etched on his face as he watched Lane. As if Lane were to blame for his wife's actions. Cait switched her gaze to Lane. The stunned look on his face as he stared at his wife aroused Cait's sympathy. Marilee sat hunched over on the sofa, her body flinching under the impact of Justin's words. Cait could feel the pain and wretched suffering of the other woman. Pity drove her to say, "The money was supposed to be mine, Justin, and I want to forget the whole thing."

"She stole the money," Justin said curtly. "She's a thief."

"Marilee must have had a good reason." Turning to her, Cait urged, "Tell Justin. He'll understand."

"Your confidence is misplaced," Justin said. "I certainly will not understand theft."

Marilee began to cry, ugly, gulping sounds that tore at Cait's ears and heart. Varying expressions of distaste covered the men's faces. None made a move toward Marilee. Her harsh sobbing filled the room until Cait could no longer stand it. "This is cruel," she flared, storming across the room to sit on the sofa and put her arm around the crumpled, weeping woman. "Don't pay any attention to Justin," Cait said gently. "When he gets upset, he says things. Once he calms down, he can be quite reasonable. For whatever reason you needed the money, we can work this out. The money's not worth crying about," she said as the woman sobbed harder.

Cait rubbed Marilee's shoulder and clasped her hands. "There's no need, we can work this out." Cait looked helplessly at Justin. He stared impassively back at her. "Justin," she beseeched, "this isn't necessary."

"Keep out of it, Cait," he said, his voice savage.

"You're the one who told me to come in here. I'm not going to keep out of it. It was my money, and I have the right to decide what's going to be done. The three of you can quit acting like hanging judges, because there's not going to be a lynching today." Her arm tightening around Marilee's shoulders, Cait stared defiantly at Justin. An odd expression gleamed in her husband's eyes. It was gone before she could identify it. She lifted her chin. Justin couldn't make her back down.

"Lane?" Justin questioned in a quiet voice.

Cait felt Marilee go rigid. "Lane has nothing to say about it, either," Cait said quickly.

Lane expelled a long breath of air. A crooked smile played across his mouth as he looked at Justin. "How did you know it was me?" When Justin merely shrugged, Lane said, "I suppose it was easier to believe I'd steal the money than that Marilee would. Why accuse her?"

Justin looked at Hank. When his uncle remained silent, Justin reluctantly spoke. "We had no proof, and Hank didn't think you'd own up to it. We hoped—" he hesitated "—we knew you wouldn't let Marilee suffer the blame."

"Now what?" Lane asked.

"You heard Cait," Justin said. "Her money. She decides." His face gave little of his thoughts away. Only his eyes hinted of his pain and disappointment. And his body braced for Cait's decision.

Hank wouldn't meet Cait's gaze. He looked shrunken and shriveled, as if he'd aged twenty years overnight.

Marilee shook off Cait's arm and edged away. The expression on Lane's face was half cocky, half fearful.

It was evident all four of them expected Cait to exact punishing revenge. She thought of all the cutting remarks she'd endured from Lane and Marilee, their efforts to make her life miserable. I owe them, she wanted to shout. They never made me welcome, they wanted to drive me away... She forced words from her dry mouth. "Is there any money left?"

"Why? Your rich daddy want it?" Lane asked in a snide voice.

"Be happy my rich daddy has nothing to do with this. He has little patience with common criminals, family or not."

Justin started to speak, then compressed his lips in a firm line.

Lane's bravado disintegrated. "I opened a new bank account and most of it's in there. The rest... I suppose you'll insist on taking Marilee's new earrings and the palomino."

"I'll select a local charity, and you will give the money in the bank to it. I don't want the earrings or the horse." Her scornful look swept the room, and then Cait turned on her heel and walked out the door.

"I thought I'd find you here."

"Go away. I don't want to talk to you." Cait tightened the cinch strap on Rosie. "Rutherfords and Valentines don't rate very high on my list of favorite people right now."

"You're a Valentine," Justin said blandly.

She ignored that. "Every single one of you," she said, pulling down the left stirrup, "was absolutely, positively convinced I was going to call in the law and have Lane locked away for the rest of his life." She looped the right rein around Rosie's neck, transferring both reins to her left hand. "It's one thing to believe I'm capable of petty behavior such as throwing Marilee's pudding on the floor—" not trusting her lower lip to refrain from childishly wobbling, she kept her back to Justin "—but you all expected me to be vicious and vindictive, without an ounce of compassion. How do you think that makes me feel?" She vaulted into the saddle.

Justin's hand closed around her ankle. "I expect it makes you feel about the same as I felt when I discovered you believed I was the kind of husband who didn't give a damn if his wife starved." Stepping back, he swatted Rosie's rump, and the horse sprang from the yard.

"It's not the same thing at all," Cait shouted into the wind. An hour later, she continued to insist the situations were quite different. Not that anyone agreed with her. Rosie had long ago quit pricking back her ears to listen, and Nick had abandoned her almost as soon as she'd started her ride. Topping a small hill, Cait had looked back to see the old dog returning in a slow lope to Justin's side. Justin had waved. She'd pretended she hadn't seen him.

Sitting relaxed in the saddle, her body swaying with the mare's easy gait, Cait continued her one-sided dialogue. If Justin was so gung ho to have her be responsible for her own actions, then it stood to reason he would expect her to support herself once she'd left his roof. There was no comparison between the way Justin had totally misjudged her and his silly little grievance. She had a right to her hurt feelings. He didn't.

She nudged Rosie farther up into the trees, barely noticing the squirrel hurling invectives at her. Justin's problem was that he was too accustomed to being in charge. Nobody assigned him to be her keeper. For all he knew, she might have done as Marilee suggested and turned to her father for money.

Marilee couldn't know that asking Rafe Montgomery for money meant inviting him to run your life. While she couldn't deny that her three older sisters appeared content with their wealthy, upper-crust, Rafe-selected husbands, Cait had had different aspirations almost from birth. She'd fought private schools, snobby colleges and ballet lessons. The only battle she'd won was riding lessons. She'd taken them for three years before her parents learned she'd enrolled in Western-style riding rather than English.

A jay squawked overhead. If he was ridiculing her, she couldn't blame him. For all her puny efforts at revolting against the establishment, she'd ended up the perfect debutante. Skilled at everything important in her mother's circle. And absolutely worthless to a man like Justin.

And so busy asserting her independence and difference from the rest of her family, she hadn't even considered Justin's viewpoint. Values like honesty, reliability and decency provided the cornerstones of his life. He practiced proper stewardship of his land, kindness to animals and unfailing justice to all. Justin wasn't just an incredibly sexy cowboy. He was a good man who'd married the woman he slept with, kept his word, honored his commitments and took care of his family.

And what was she? Marilee's words rang in her head. She was a disaster. Vaguely aware something cold and damp had been powdering her face for the past few minutes, Cait roused herself from her self-pitying preoccupation. Large fluffy snowflakes floated to the ground, encasing her in a world of downy white. Cait caught a flake on the tip of her tongue.

Rosie threw up her head and stopped abruptly. Cait leaned down and patted the mare's neck. "Now what? There aren't any bulls up here." She nudged Rosie, but the mare snorted and refused to budge. Cait looked over the mare's ears and caught her breath.

Barely visible through a curtain of falling snow stood a mountain lion, motionless in a dark clump of junipers and pines. Cait and the large tawny cat stared at each other; then swiftly and silently the animal vanished.

When she'd first come to the valley, Justin had told her what to do if she ever came upon a mountain lion. She wasn't to run, but to look large and let the big cat know she wasn't food. Justin had assured her that in most cases the mountain lion would be more leery of her than the other way around. Cait had never questioned before what Justin meant by "in most cases". Now she said, in what she hoped was a confident but calm voice, "We're not food, Mr. Lion. You'll have to find another restaurant." Unzipping her jacket, she held it wide open, her hands outstretched. Rosie trembled between her knees. Cait slowly backed the mare away from where she'd last seen the mountain lion.

It took all Cait's strength and skill to keep Rosie from bolting. When they emerged from the trees onto a rough dirt road, Cait judged they'd left the large cat far behind, and wheeling Rosie about, she let the mare have her head. Pounding down the rugged path eventually exorcised the demons from Rosie's memory, and the mare responded to Cait's reining her in to a walk. Cait looked back over her shoulder, but there was no sign of any mountain lion.

She began to wonder if she'd actually seen the elusive predator, or if what she'd thought was a mountain lion had been a trick of light combined with an overactive imagination brought on by Rosie's behavior. Cait rubbed

Rosie's neck. "Well, girl, did you get spooked by your shadow and did I get spooked by you? Did we really see a mountain lion, or was he merely an illusion?"

Maybe her whole life was an illusion. Thinking her parents loved her in spite of their busy lives that had no place for her. Thinking she could fit into Justin's family. Thinking she belonged on the ranch. Thinking she could make Justin love her.

Cait shook her head. She wasn't giving up yet. Christmas was still a few days away. Her anniversary came two days later. Plenty of time remained to win Justin's love. And if she failed, there was always her ace in the hole. Now that Lane had been caught stealing, Justin would be even more appreciative that Cait had come back to save the ranch for him.

Rosie halted at an intersection of two roads and tossed her head. Uneasily, Cait noted the soft, fluffy snow-flakes had been replaced by hard, stinging pellets that fell increasingly faster and thicker. If the sun had been shining, it would have dipped below the mountains now. On the nicest days, night came earlier to the foothills where Cait was riding. On a snowy afternoon like this, an early, gloomy dusk swallowed up the tall pines and sprawling junipers. "C'mon, Rosie," Cait said, "let's go back."

Crossing her hands on the saddle horn, Cait stood in the stirrups and looked around. There existed one tiny little problem. She didn't have the faintest idea in which direction to go.

CHAPTER NINE

UNFORTUNATELY, neither did Rosie. "Horses are supposed to know how to find their way home," Cait said, struggling to dissuade the mare from continuing down the road in the direction they'd been traveling. The one thing Cait knew was that that direction couldn't possibly be the way back to the ranch house. Rosie danced skittishly, shaking her head, but Cait finally managed to turn the mare back the way they'd come.

Cait had no more desire than did Rosie to pass the spot where she might have seen a mountain lion, but common sense told her retracing their footsteps would be the best means of finding their way home. It was a theory worthy of Einstein. Except the ever-increasing, rapidly falling snow had covered their tracks, and Cait couldn't find the place where they'd exited the woods and come onto this road. Nor did she recognize what little of the road she could see. "Face it, Caitlin Valentine," she said out loud. "You have stupidly gotten yourself hopelessly lost." That ought to impress Justin.

Tidbits of survival lore ran through her head. Unfortunately, the high school she'd attended had concentrated on urban survival. A smidgen of an article she'd read somewhere came back to her. When lost and stranded in a snowstorm, a person was supposed to burn her car's spare tire to produce a column of smoke that could be seen for miles. Considering the circumstances, it wasn't the most helpful of advice.

The mare shied at something beside the road. "Now, Rosie," Cait said in a soothing voice, "quit seeing ghosts and goblins everywhere." Rosie jerked her head, and Cait had a strong suspicion the mare was well aware Cait was every bit as nervous as she was. Halting the mare, Cait dismounted. Maybe if she led Rosie, the horse would be less skittish. Head bowed against the blowing snow, Cait plowed ahead, practically dragging the recalcitrant mare.

Finally, Rosie refused to advance one more step. Planting her feet firmly in the road, the mare turned her head and pricked her ears in the direction they'd come from. Cait stared into the night and the swirling snow, seeing nothing, but imagining an army of mountain lions and who knew what else sneaking up on her. Already nervous, Rosie's sudden loud whinny startled Cait into loosening her grip on the reins. Rosie jerked the reins free and took off down the road at a gallop.

Cait took off her hat and slammed it to the ground in a fit of temper, borrowing some choice words from Justin's sometimes colorful vocabulary. "You are the world's stupidest horse," she hollered. "If you don't get back here immediately, from now on I'm riding Double Looney." To her amazement, the threat worked.

Rosie came clip-clopping back. The mare was not alone.

Cait retrieved her hat from the ground and carefully brushed off the snow and smoothed the hat back into shape.

Justin waited. When Cait finally put on her hat and looked up in acknowledgment of his presence, he handed her Rosie's reins. "Nasty weather for a hike."

Cait wondered aloud if Colorado had the death penalty. "Not that a jury of my peers would find me guilty of murder. My peers being other women who have to put up with insensitive husbands who make fun of their wives when they land in a predicament not of their making." Cait swung up on Rosie. "If it's of any interest to you, I did not fall off, and I'm quite sure I won't be crippled for life.''

Justin turned Nighthawk in the direction he'd come from. "I knew you were okay when I heard you swearing like a trooper. What happened? Why were you headed that way?''

"What way?'' Cait asked cautiously.

"Away from the ranch. I managed to follow your trail pretty much through the woods, but lost it before you hit the road. I would have gone the other way, but Nighthawk was determined to come this way. He tracks like a dog, so I let him have his head, but I'd about decided he was wrong this time when he started whinnying. Sure enough, here came Rosie to greet us.''

If Justin was trying to hide his amusement, he wasn't trying hard enough. "I suppose you think I was lost?''

"No, I don't think it," Justin drawled.

Meaning he knew darned well she'd been lost. Even Rosie, now trotting meekly beside the black gelding, had more brains than Cait when it came to finding her way home. "We saw a mountain lion and Rosie panicked. By the time I got her settled down, we'd been all over the countryside. That and the snow were enough to disorient anyone.''

After a bit, Justin asked, "Where did you see this mountain lion?''

"Why do you even bother to ask? I can tell by your voice you don't believe me.''

"I believe you saw something. A deer, or maybe a coyote.''

"But not a mountain lion.''

"Cait, people who have lived here for years have never seen a mountain lion. Hell, I've lived here for twenty years and I've only seen one once.''

"Which proves conclusively I couldn't have seen one, because I don't even belong here." The road turned, and Cait had to shout the words into an increasing wind.

Justin hunched over his horse, peering ahead into the dark. Cait huddled into her jacket for warmth. Annoyed as she was at Justin, she was grateful for his presence. The thickly falling snow cut them off from the rest of the world as they plodded along the road.

Snow drifted down inside her collar and clung to her eyelashes. Cait lifted her head to ask Justin how much farther and forgot her miserable state. "Justin, look."

Justin brought his black gelding to a halt. Rosie was anxious for the barn, but Cait held the mare at Nighthawk's side. Ahead, red and green and yellow and blue jewels glowed through the falling snow.

"The Christmas lights on the sun-room," Cait said softly. "Guiding us home." She didn't know if Justin heard her. After a minute, he made a clicking sound to Nighthawk, and they headed in.

In the barn, Cait swung down off Rosie and found Justin at her back.

"I'll take care of Rosie," he said. "You get on up to the house and let Hank know you're okay. He'll pretend he doesn't care, but he was worried sick about you."

"Well, sure, I must owe him two million dollars at gin."

Justin tipped up her chin. "You are all right?"

"Yes. A little cold and a little wet is all." Cait focused on his nose. "And a little embarrassed. So much for my horse skills. Rosie tried to tell me I was going the wrong direction."

"All of us go the wrong direction at times." Hands on her shoulders, he turned her around so she faced the barn door. "Now get going. And take a hot shower. I don't want an ice cube in my bed tonight."

At least he wanted her in his bed. Even if they both knew marrying her was the wrongest direction Justin had ever gone.

"C'mon, lazybones, rise and shine."

Cait hated people who were cheerful in the morning. Muttering, she clamped a pillow over her head. A cold hand snaked under the covers and grabbed her bare hip. Letting out a piercing shriek, she threw the pillow in the direction of the man attached to the hand. "You really like to live dangerously," she snarled, giving him a dirty look.

Unfazed, Justin grinned down at her. "Get your behind out of bed or you're not going to have time for breakfast, much less coffee."

"If you had an ounce of compassion, you'd go away and leave me alone to recuperate from my horrible ordeal of last night."

"Recuperate later," said her coldhearted husband, his hands resting on his hips. "Now you have to get up and help me feed cattle. I'm shorthanded."

Cait secured the blankets around her neck. "Why?"

"Lane and Marilee made a last-minute decision to spend Christmas with Doreen and Cullen. They left last night."

"Are they coming back?"

"Probably. You have a problem with that?"

"Not if Lane coming back means you won't keep trying to get me up in the middle of the night to feed stupid cows."

"Trying?" Justin cocked an arrogant brow. "Let me put it this way, Mrs. Valentine. If you aren't out of that bed in ten seconds, you're not only going without breakfast and coffee, you're going to be out feeding cows while wearing not much more than a coat and boots."

His grin was more leer. "I might appreciate the scenery, but the cows won't give a hoot, and it's pretty damned chilly out there."

It was more than chilly; it was darn cold. Cait shivered ostentatiously and made a chattering sound with her teeth, neither of which impressed her husband as he slung the last bale of hay onto the truck. Of course, he probably was warm, having worked up a sweat flexing all those rippling muscles as he tossed around the bales. Not that Cait could actually see the muscles hidden by Justin's warm clothing. She didn't need to see them. Her imagination had no trouble supplying the necessary visuals.

Justin opened the passenger door of the pickup. "Scoot over. You can drive."

Cait looked at the gearshift and managed to bite back the retort that she certainly couldn't. She'd driven a manual shift before. In driver's training. Back in high school. Surely that sort of thing was like riding a bicycle—a skill one never forgot. She scooted over.

"Hell, you haven't driven a pickup before, have you?" Justin read her hesitation with unerring accuracy.

She might have known a little ignorance wasn't going to excuse her from the chores.

In the pasture fifteen minutes later, Justin stood outside the open truck door and yelled, "Okay, nothing to it. I'm going to get in back and toss down the hay. You can see where we fed yesterday, so drive along the same path in a giant circle. The key is to drive real slow so I have plenty of time to break up the bales and spread the hay. Don't worry about the cows. They're more interested in food than the pickup. They'll stay out of your way." He slammed the door shut.

Cait felt the pickup sway as Justin jumped up in back. He slapped his hand on the top of the truck cab in a signal for her to start. Nick, who was balanced on top of the bales, barked sharply. Cait reached for the gear-shift lever.

Driving the truck was a cinch. Cait could smell the broken-up hay bales, not to mention the cows. Above the sound of the engine, cows mooed, Nick barked and the hay hit the ground. Feeling like a real cowhand tooling around the rough pastureland, she switched on the radio. A country-and-western station blared forth. "Hell," she said, trying the word out loud. It sounded so westernish, she tried it again. "Hell, all I need is a chaw of tobaccy."

Listening to some cowboy crooner lament wild city women, Cait failed to see the dip in the pasture. Luckily she was wearing her seat belt, or she'd have put her head through the roof of the truck. Justin didn't yell so he obviously was used to a rough ride. She joined in the song on the radio with the chorus, wailing out the words at the top of her lungs. These country guys sure did a lot of singing about falling in with the wrong kind of women. Whatever happened to songs about cows?

The route she was following around the pasture was more of an oblong than a circle. As she rounded the far end, Cait looked back to check on the cows strung out behind her, feeding. There weren't any cows strung out behind her. Most of the cows were bunched halfway up the pasture. Craning her head, Cait checked the ground behind her. No piles of green-tinted hay trailed after the truck. She looked in her rearview mirror. Nick rode the diminished stack of hay in solitary splendor. There was no sign of Justin. Cait looked again at the milling cattle. Two cows moved, revealing a pair of long, denim-clad legs lying lifeless on the ground.

Cait stomped down on the accelerator and raced across the pasture, scattering cows with the blaring horn. Forgetting the clutch, she slammed on the brakes, and the truck bucked to a halt. A few determined cows ignored her and continued to inhale the scattered hay. Cait slapped their rumps, shoving them out of her way. She fell to her knees at Justin's side. "Justin! Justin, are you okay? Open your eyes, look at me!"

"I'd rather strangle you," he said in a deliberate voice. "What did I say, Cait? Drive slow. Slow, I said. I know I said drive slow. I'll bet I said drive slow five or six times." His eyelids shot up. "So why the hell were you tearing across the pasture as if you were entered in the Indianapolis 500?"

Cait sagged back on her heels. "Are you hurt?" she asked cautiously.

"No, I am not hurt." He made no move to get up.

Cait gave him a tentative smile. "Just mad?"

He considered that. "I guess you could say I'm a little annoyed." He stared up at the blue sky. "It shouldn't have been that difficult. You drive, slowly," he said, practically shouting the last word, "and I dump out the hay. I've been feeding cattle for twenty-some winters, and this is the first time I've been bucked out of the pickup."

"So only your male pride is hurt," Cait scoffed.

Justin heaved a loud sigh. "I really wish you hadn't said that, Cait."

Before Cait could ask why, Justin came up off the ground, grabbing her around her thighs and sweeping her off her feet.

She ended up facedown over Justin's shoulders. "Justin," she screeched, "put me down this instant." He put her down. She landed on her back on a scratchy bed of hay bales. At a quick word from Justin, Nick leaped over her supine body and jumped to the ground.

Justin unbuckled his belt and reached for the zipper of his jeans.

Cait's eyes widened. "Justin, it's broad daylight. We're supposed to be feeding the cows."

"The damned cows can wait. What can't wait is teaching you the proper respect for your husband." His mouth stopped Cait's giggles.

Sometime later, Cait brushed the hay off her back and straightened her clothes. "Honestly, Justin." She zipped her jacket back up. "At least I know you weren't injured."

"Honestly, Cait," he mimicked. "At least you nicely apologized for trying to kill me."

"I wasn't trying to kill you." She gave him a sideways glance. "And the methods you used to coerce that apology out of me were absolutely reprehensible."

Justin picked a piece of hay out of her hair and handed her her hat. "I didn't hear you complaining at the time."

"Everybody knows when a person goes stark, raving mad, the safest thing is to humor him."

"Must've worked. I'm in a better humor," Justin said absently, as he jumped down from the pickup bed and looked around. "Do you see my hat anywhere?"

Cait spotted the hat first. If she could have hidden it, she would have. Unfortunately, she couldn't figure out how to remove it from under the right front wheel of the pickup without Justin noticing.

"I'm surprised you let me come." Her arms loaded with greens, Cait staggered up the hill in Justin's wake, plowing through fresh powder over ankle-deep crusted snow. "Aren't you afraid I might knock over the headstones?"

"I thought it would be more convenient. When I murder you, I won't have to drag your body so far."

"I didn't run over it on purpose," Cait said defensively. "I thought you were unconscious or—" she swallowed "—dead or something. How many times do I have to tell you I'm sorry about your precious old hat? I offered to buy you a new one."

"Which clearly exposes your ignorance. That hat is irreplaceable. Do you know how long it took me to get it exactly how I wanted it?"

"Yes, I do. You've been telling me for hours." Stopping to breathe deeply of the crisp air, Cait looked around the small old cemetery that sprawled up and around the hillside. The setting was wrong for quarreling. "I'm sorry, I shouldn't have said that, Justin. And honestly, I am sorry about driving over your hat. We both should have known putting me behind the wheel of the pickup while you were feeding the cattle was begging for a disaster to happen."

"If you think you can get out of helping me the rest of the week, think again. You're going to have to wreck more than my hat before I'll let you sleep in in the morning."

"Justin," Cait said, outraged, "I wasn't trying to get out of work. I was trying to apologize."

"I know." He gave her a lopsided smile. "I was teasing you." His grin turned to a ferocious scowl. "But next time, when I say slow, I mean slow."

"I think you made your point this morning."

Justin raised both eyebrows. "It's good to know there is a way to train you."

Cait blushed warmly and changed the subject before Justin became depraved enough to demonstrate his training methods in a cemetery. "I've always wondered why your parents aren't buried here."

Justin unlatched the gate in the wrought-iron enclosure around the Rutherford burial plot. "Dad was an only child of older parents. They wanted their son buried near them in Iowa, and Hank said Mom and Dad ought to be together.'' Justin brushed snow off the nearest tombstone. "I guess it doesn't much matter."

"Wherever your parents are, I believe they know how you're doing, and they must be very proud of you," Cait said softly. "I'm sure they're happy to see how you and Hank care for each other." On her knees in the snow, she arranged the greens, tying a bright red bow on top.

"I was ten when my parents died in a car accident. With Dad in the air force, we'd lived all over the place. Even if Hank was Mom's brother, I'd only met him twice, but he and Marie came out on the first plane they could get on. Hank told me he had no intention of taking the place of Mom and Dad, but he and Marie wanted me to live with them for as long as I wanted."

His voice was pitched low, but Cait heard the emotion behind the words. "You were the son he and Marie never had."

"Marie and the baby died only two years after my parents." Justin brushed snow from Marie's and Mary Amanda's white marble headstone. "I heard talk. People said Hank was crazy to raise me by himself. Hank told me to ignore the talk, that he and I were family and family stuck together."

The greenery blurred in front of Cait, and a painful lump swelled in the back of her throat. "After Marie died, you were Hank's main reason for living." She forced a lighthearted note into her voice. "He told me the other day that even if you are an insolent pup, he's kind of proud of you."

"I'd rather be an insolent pup than an old buzzard," Justin said, his automatic response honed through years of practice.

When she'd first arrived at the ranch, the name-calling had horrified Cait until she'd realized it denoted deep affection, not rancor. "I feel badly Hank decided he'd better not risk coming," she said. "This will be the first time since Marie died that he isn't paying her a Christmas visit. I suggested he could sit in the truck, but he said that would make him feel worse."

"Marie would understand." Justin handed Cait more greens.

A nuthatch called from a nearby stand of pines. Cait finished arranging the pine boughs and stood up, knocking the snow from her knees. "I love this cemetery. The fancy stones. The old wooden markers. There's a sense of history here, and family." She indicated the tombstones around her. "Your family, for instance. The first Henry, who came out here in the 1880s, bought land from one of the early German colonizers and started the ranch. He was your great-great-grandfather. Your great-grandfather worked the ranch, your grandfather and now Hank and you. Rosita and Querida and the other mining boomtowns in the valley were a flash in the pan, fading away when the precious ores petered out, but the Rutherfords have staying power."

"I see Hank has been stuffing your head with family lore."

"Don't you dare tell me it's all another myth."

Justin laughed. "Not exactly a myth, but an expurgated version of what really happened. Young Henry was the younger son of a wealthy family back in England, and he lived off the regular allowance his family sent him. The only thing Henry worked at was hunting, drinking and carousing."

"He bought the ranch," Cait pointed out.

"Not exactly." Justin secured the gate behind them and followed Cait down the slope to the pickup. "It seems ol' Henry cast his eye and few other parts in the direction of a pretty German *Fräulein*, and he married her, strongly persuaded to do so by a loaded shotgun held by her German papa. A man didn't mess around with respectable women back then.'' Justin shrugged. ''They had four kids, and he lived to age seventy-two, a pretty ripe old age in those days, so things must have worked out. Where he came from, younger sons usually lost out on property, and Emile was an only child, so Henry didn't do too badly, gaining himself a large hunk of land and a woman who was undoubtedly raised from birth to be a proper *Hausfrau.*''

Two men forced to marry where they didn't love. ''Henry did better than you,'' Cait said.

''That's debatable. There's a picture of Emile in one of the old family albums.'' He opened the pickup door for Cait. ''My taste in women doesn't run to short, blond and plump.''

Cait trailed a finger down Justin's chest and peered flirtatiously up at him from under lowered lashes. ''What does your taste in women run to, cowboy?''

Holding the door open with his body, he rested his hands on her hips and aimed a slow, sexy smile at her. ''Tall and slender with long legs, chopped off black hair and curves in all the right places.''

If Justin could bottle his smile, he'd make a fortune. Of course, Cait would have to buy all the bottles. Ignoring her racing pulse, she reminded him, ''You said it was debatable if Henry did better. Meaning you think in some ways he did.''

The skin crinkled around Justin's eyes. ''Damned right he did. You can tell by looking at Emile's picture.''

''Tell what?'' Cait pushed her bottom lip out in an exaggerated pout. ''That she had secret recipes for dumplings and sauerkraut?''

"No." Justin leaned down and gently nipped her lower lip with his teeth. "That she never, ever ran over her husband's hat." Laughing, he moved quickly to put the open door between them.

Cait gave a ladylike sniff and stepped up into the pickup. An opportunity for revenge would come.

In the driver's seat, Justin switched on the ignition. "Why the sudden interest in family history?"

"Hank talks about it all the time while we're playing gin. No doubt to distract me." The air in the cab suddenly seemed filled with tension. Cait frowned at Justin. "What?"

Justin gave her a quick look and then locked his gaze on the road ahead. "Hank's accident brought it home to him that he won't always be around. Suddenly he's a lot more concerned about what will happen once he's gone."

Cait thought of Hank's talk about wills. "I know. I keep telling him he's too mean to die."

After a long pause, Justin said, "I told him not to say anything to you."

Cait went very still. Justin knew Hank was threatening to leave the ranch half in Lane's control. He must have guessed Cait had returned as part of a bargain with Hank to keep the control of the ranch in Justin's hands. Maybe her ace in the hole was only a deuce. Instead of Justin feeling obligated to her, maybe he thought she owed him, and her staying until their anniversary was a fair repayment of her debt. She stared down at the hands curled tightly in her lap. "We discussed it, yes. I wasn't aware Hank had said anything to you."

Justin gave a snort of disgust. "If by 'said anything' you mean Hank's been nagging me since he broke his hip, yes, you could say he said something." He scowled out the windshield. "I told him to keep his big mouth shut. I should have known he wouldn't listen." It was a little late for Justin to plead ignorance. Cait opened her mouth to tell him so, when he continued, "You should have told Hank to mind his own damned business."

"I wanted to, but you have to admit, it really is his business." It was Hank's will and his family's ranch.

"Don't tell me you fell for that line," Justin said tightly. "Ensuring there will be another generation to run the family ranch is not the best reason I can think of to have a baby."

"A baby," Cait echoed faintly.

"And it's not true anyway. Lane and Marilee will probably have kids one of these days. The truth is, Hank has a hankering to play grandpa and he figures he needs my kids for that."

Justin's baby. The picture of Justin as a baby in his mother's arms flashed into Cait's mind. What would it be like to hold Justin's baby? Impulsively she turned to tell Justin she'd love to have his baby.

"I told Hank—" Justin's knuckles were white against the steering wheel as he manhandled the pickup around a sharp curve "—there's no way he's going to manipulate me into giving him a grandkid. If he brings it up to you again, tell him flat out. No babies."

Justin's words told Cait everything. He'd made a commitment and he would let her stay. After all, any woman could sleep in a man's bed, live in his house. An icy lump formed in Cait's stomach. But when it came to having his babies, raising his children, a man had certain minimum standards. Standards Cait could never hope to meet. Tears pricked at the back of her eyelids. Never to hold Justin's baby...

As they passed through town, a house elaborately decorated for the holidays caught Cait's eye. Christmas was three days away, her anniversary five days away. Was she a quitter or was she Rafe Montgomery's daughter? She had five days to convince Justin she was the perfect mother for his unborn children.

Cait felt like tearing her hair out by the roots. Why couldn't these cookbook authors write in plain English? She was fairly certain she knew what simmer meant, but sauté? Giblets? And what the heck was a double boiler? When she'd casually mentioned her proposed menu to Mrs. Courtney, the housekeeper had breathed a sigh of relief and given her approval. Simple but tasty, she'd said. Simple maybe for Mrs. Courtney. Cait wished she'd read the recipes a little more attentively before the older woman had left for Denver. The thing about egg salad was it required so few ingredients and no measuring. Just toss cooked eggs and stuff together and there you were.

Maybe she ought to listen to Sarah and fix spaghetti. No, anybody could open up a jar and have spaghetti. To prove a point, a wife cooked a turkey and all the trimmings, not to mention chocolate pie made according to Sarah's special recipe. Cait had successfully fixed a chocolate pie a half-dozen times or more during the past two years. If the way to a man's heart was through his stomach, that pie was going to put Cait in the express lane to Justin's heart.

A loud rustle diverted her. "Lucy, you get away from those packages." Cait hustled across the room and snagged the kitten from under the Christmas tree. A shredded red bow dangled from the kitten's claws. "You, young lady," Cait said severely, "are a big, big nuisance. I'm beginning to think, instead of rescuing you from the eagle, I saved the eagle from you. I rewrapped that package once already." She shook her finger in the kitten's face. "Santa Claus is watching you." That would teach Cait to wrap up a toy with catnip in it and put it under the tree. By the time Cait had wised up and removed the package, Lucy had discovered the unmitigated joys of playing with wrapping paper and ribbon.

Not content with mauling the packages Cait had wrapped, Lucy had zeroed in on the elegant and expensive wrapping on the packages from Cait's sisters. Shelly, before joining her husband's family in Florida for their annual family get-together, had sent her usual gift-wrapped envelope, stock in something selected by an associate of Shelly's banker husband. Allison had sent another place setting of heavy·silverware, and Tracy had sent another place setting of ornate porcelain. The last two gifts would have been efficiently ordered by phone and mailed by the store before the sisters and their families flew to Vermont for their annual Christmas ski trip.

With Lucy's package hidden high in a closet, only three other packages sat under the tree—a chew toy for Nick and large framed photographs for Hank and Justin. Cait didn't intend to repeat her earlier mistake of showering the men with presents they neither needed or wanted.

No stockings hung in front of the fireplace. Two years ago after Justin mentioned Marie had hung Christmas stockings, Cait had ordered three large needlepointed stockings with her, Justin's and Hank's names on them. She'd hung the stockings a week before Christmas, and Christmas Eve she'd sneaked out of bed and filled the men's with trinkets and sundries. Christmas morning she'd kept away from the living room long enough to allow the men to fill her stocking. Her Christmas stocking had remained miserably bare.

The entire Christmas Day had been miserable. Pretending it didn't matter she'd received only flannel pajamas and a cookbook, Cait's hurt feelings had rapidly mushroomed until she'd exploded in a king-sized tantrum, accusing Justin of everything from marrying her for her money to deliberately making her unhappy so she'd go away. He'd called her spoiled and childish. The argument had escalated from there.

They hadn't been on speaking terms that afternoon when they'd gone to Marilee and Lane's for Christmas dinner. Marilee had shown off a portion of her gifts from Lane and his parents, too many for Cait even to recall. Each one had been a spike driven into her heart.

She'd refused to speak to Justin the next day. The following day, their anniversary, expecting flowers and gifts from Justin in atonement for his transgressions on Christmas Day, Cait had decided to be magnanimous and forgive him. At Cait's request, Mrs. Courtney had prepared an extra-special dinner. Cait had set the table with candles and a formal tablecloth she'd found in the linen closet and placed new silver and porcelain at Justin's place.

At 7:00 p.m., Justin had called to say they'd just finished doctoring a sick cow. He and Hank were at Lane's, and he hoped she'd gone ahead and eaten. They were discussing the cow so Marilee had fixed them dinner and he'd be home late.

Marilee had been at the house that afternoon while Cait was setting the table. Marilee knew it was Cait's anniversary. Cait had thought about that awhile. Then she had thought about Justin forgetting their first anniversary. Then she had packed. Everyone was going to be very sorry they'd treated her so badly. Justin would come tearing after her, begging her forgiveness.

And pigs and cows and horses would all fly.

CHAPTER TEN

NOISE from across the room told Cait Lucy had returned to her playground beneath the Christmas tree. Cait crawled under the tree in search of the kitten. A piteous meow sent her gaze upward. Inches from the top, Lucy clung precariously to the trunk of the scrawny tree. "I suppose you expect me to help you down."

"Snooping through your Christmas packages?"

Cait banged her head on the pine branch over her head. "Quit sneaking up on me!"

Justin plucked the kitten from the tree. "Looking for this little lady? This isn't the first time I've found her where she shouldn't be. Trouble is her middle name."

Scooting from beneath the tree, Cait sat back on her heels. Justin loomed over her, the small cat lost in his large hands. "Don't say she takes after me," Cait warned.

He grinned. "A little touchy on that subject, are you?" He one-handedly pulled Cait to her feet. And noticed the cookbook she held. "You're serious about cooking dinner on Christmas, aren't you?"

"Worried I'll put arsenic in the stuffing?"

"I'll let you taste everything first," Justin said absently, frowning at the half-dozen packages at the base of the tree.

Cait said hastily, "It's just a little something "

He transferred his gaze to her. "Lane called this morning. In their rush to pack, they forgot to bring back the file. He told me where it was, and I picked it up from their place. It's on the bed."

"Oh." She took the kitten from Justin's hands.

"I didn't read it."

Her eyes flew to his face. "Why not?"

"I don't pry into my wife's life," Justin said in a level voice. "I don't care how worried Hank was about you. He was wrong to hire a private detective to watch you." He hesitated. "Although I admit to a certain curiosity, you're under no obligation to tell me what you've been doing for two years or why you were waiting tables for a living."

"What are you curious about?" Cait curled the kitten's tail around her finger.

"For one thing, how your parents felt about your working as a waitress."

"There's nothing disgraceful about waiting tables for a living," Cait said evasively.

"I never said there was, but it's not exactly post-debutante behavior. Your parents must have been less than thrilled."

Cait couldn't meet his eyes. "The subject didn't exactly come up." She set Lucy down on the floor.

A long silence greeted her reluctant admission. "I see," Justin finally said. "Why don't you tell me exactly what you did say? Just in case the subject ever comes up—" he sardonically underlined the last few words "—in a conversation I'm having with your father or mother."

"At first I told them I'd decided to take a few college courses so I had to live in Colorado Springs during the week."

"And on the weekend?"

She avoided looking at him. "They sort of thought I came back here."

"You said 'at first'. What did you tell them later?"

"That I was spending all my time in Colorado Springs."

"And what did they 'sort of' think then?" Justin asked grimly.

"They might have kind of jumped to the conclusion that we were temporarily separated because you weren't thrilled about my going back to school."

"I take it you didn't bother to correct their asinine conclusion." His calm voice couldn't disguise the fact that Justin was seething with outrage.

Cait thought of and discarded several million excuses. "I won't insult you by attempting to justify my behavior," she said. "The truth is—"

"The truth!" Justin snapped. "The truth is you were annoyed because you'd built up in your mind this image of your perfect Christmas, and I failed to produce it. I might have come a hell of a lot closer if you'd bothered to give me a hint or two of what you were expecting."

"It wasn't—"

"Just Christmas," he finished savagely. "I'm well aware what sent you running away the night of our anniversary. You were furious because I chose to deal with a ranch emergency rather than come home to you. Life was always black and white with you. There was never any gray middle ground. You were a spoiled little brat, always insisting I choose between you and the ranch."

"I'm sorry, I—"

"Why? Because your little scheme didn't work?"

"No, I—"

"You thought I'd come rushing up to Colorado Springs and fall on bended knees, begging you to forgive me."

"Justin, I . . ." The truth couldn't be denied.

"That's what the waitress business was about. You were turning the screw. Poor little girl, driven out in the middle of the cold night and abandoned by her neglectful, uncaring husband, forced to work her little manicured fingers to the bone. You didn't run home to Daddy because that would have ruined your piteous little scenario of the wronged wife living in poverty."

"Justin, no," Cait whispered, grabbing the nearest chair, the blood draining from her head. "I never—"

"The hell you didn't. You allowed your parents to think what they did because you knew how the truth would look to them. The same way it looked to you. That I was a sleazy, no-good bum of a husband who didn't bother to support his wife."

"I told you before, I didn't—"

"You've told me lots of things," he interrupted icily. "The things you didn't tell me are the ones that matter, though, aren't they? Were you ever going to tell me about your photography?"

"I've been trying to explain, but you don't make it easy."

"Hell, I'm sorry, Cait. Should I have begged you to tell me the only reason you came back is because some damned art gallery wants photographs of ranch living?"

Stunned by his conclusion, she could only stare at him.

"Or are the photographs just an excuse to get you back here and in my bed? Did you think if you reminded me what I was missing, I'd beg you to come back to me? Well, think again, Cait, because I have no intention of begging."

"No," Cait breathed in dawning awareness. "You want me to beg."

Her words brought Justin up short. After a bit, he said slowly, "Maybe you're right. Maybe I do." He wheeled and left the room.

"Rafe Montgomery's daughter doesn't beg," Cait shouted at his departing back. Justin didn't bother to turn around. The real question was, would Justin Valentine's wife beg? Cait didn't know the answer.

Cait knelt on the floor and ripped the festive Christmas paper from a large corrugated cardboard carton. Slitting the tape with her fingernails, she lifted the flaps. "Oh my gosh!" Inside the box, amid mountains of crumpled red tissue paper rested a camera lens, a tripod and a photographer's vest. "Oh my gosh," she said again. Moving aside the kitten who was halfway into the box, Cait reverently picked up the large lens. "A 35 to 350 millimeter zoom. I've been dying to have one of these."

Stunned by the expensive gift, she didn't quite know what to say. Since Justin had blown up at her yesterday, they'd coexisted in a state of remote politeness. Last night, sharing his bed, Cait hadn't known how to bridge the enormous gulf between them. She'd been tempted to reach across the wide expanse of sheet and touch his warm, bare skin in hopes he'd take her in his arms. Her hands had remained clenched at her sides. The wound she'd inflicted on Justin went too deep to be bandaged by mere physical closeness.

She'd come down to breakfast this morning prepared to find no gift for her from Justin under the tree. She hadn't been prepared for this. Awkwardly she said, "Thank you, Justin."

"The stuff is from Hank, too."

"I'm not much of a shopper," Hank said gruffly.

Cait gave him a misty-eyed smile. "You couldn't have done better," she assured him. "Thank you." Carefully returning the lens to the box, she stood up and handed the two remaining gifts from under the tree to Justin and Hank. "These aren't quite so exciting, but...Merry Christmas."

Hank opened his first. Cait's heart sank when he looked at the print a minute and then set it down on his lap without comment. Pulling out a handkerchief, he blew his nose loudly. "Damn. I got something in my eye." He held up the picture. "Take a look at this, Justin. Cait must think we have mice. She gave me something to scare them away." He blew his nose again. The photo, Justin and Nighthawk cutting cattle, captured the intense concentration on the part of man and horse.

Justin slanted Cait a quick look and tore the paper from his large rectangular gift. He cleared his throat. "This'll scare away the rats." Holding the photo out in front of him, he studied it at length before showing it to Hank. The Sangre de Cristos provided a rugged backdrop for a close-up shot of Hank, with his weathered face and sharp eyes, leaning on an old, wooden-railed corral.

"Hell," the older man said, "we ought to give that damned camera of hers to Nighthawk to stomp. What's the matter with taking pictures of wildflowers?"

"Ranch pictures are what sells," Justin said before Cait could open her mouth.

"She doesn't need to sell pictures," Hank objected. "She's got us."

Before they could argue about it, Cait interjected, "Thank you both for my Christmas present. You couldn't have made a better choice. How did you know exactly what I wanted?"

Waving his hand in his nephew's direction, Hank said, "He can tell you." Leaning on his walker, he limped from the room.

"I phoned your friend, Donald Clary," Justin said. "He made some suggestions. He also warned me it could be a long haul before you can support yourself with your photography. I guess he wasn't any happier about your being a waitress than I am.''

Cait collected the tattered remnants of gift wrap. ''I could explain why I worked as a waitress, but you clearly prefer your own version of events.''

''I'm listening.''

She gave him a long look before making up her mind. ''All right. I needed a job—''

''You didn't need a job.''

''I wanted,'' she said loudly, ''a job that allowed me free time during the day. I took classes in art and photography, and I spent a lot of daylight hours roaming the countryside wasting film. Waiting tables at night fitted my requirements better than any other job I checked out.'' She stretched a length of ribbon between her fingers. Her gaze on the ribbon, she added in a low voice, ''At first, I did expect you to come charging after me, but I never, ever waited tables in an attempt to make you feel bad or guilty.'' A long silence stretched between them. Cait forced herself to continue. ''I admit I wanted you to feel it was your fault I left, but once I realized you weren't coming after me, I wanted to prove to all of you I was capable of taking care of myself.''

''And having proved it, you came back to thumb your nose at us.''

''No,'' Cait cried, ''I came back because—'' She clapped her mouth shut. Suddenly, with the crystal clarity of hindsight, she realized that Hank had never intended to carry out his threat. Caretaker of the family ranch for decades, Hank wasn't about to leave it in any hands other than Justin's capable ones. He'd made the threat to Cait for two reasons—to see if she cared enough about Justin to supposedly save his ranch, and if she did, to try to reconcile the couple because he wanted little greatnieces and great-nephews running around the ranch. A woman born and bred on the land would never have fallen for Hank's trick. A woman born and bred on a ranch would know the land came first.

"You came back because?" Justin prodded.

Justin would be furious at his uncle if he learned how Hank had interfered. She couldn't cause trouble between the two men. Which meant she couldn't use her so-called sacrifice in coming back as a means of forcing Justin to love her. What a fool she was. Cait managed to curve her lips into a wobbly smile. "I came back because I was wrong to leave the way I did. I came back because I want us to be friends."

"I see," Justin said, starting from the room. In the doorway, he turned to study her with narrowed eyes. "I wonder what you were going to say before you changed your mind. I wonder why you really came back."

Cait pushed the hair out of her eyes with a flour-dusted hand. This was it. The showdown at the Rutherford corral. She swallowed a wild giggle. Nerves, weariness and the knowledge she'd put entirely too many eggs in one basket were making her a little crazy. Twenty-five days of living here on the ranch, attempting to prove she could fit in and would be a proper rancher's wife for Justin, and so far she'd been a dismal failure. She'd literally galloped from one disaster to another. So now it all came down to this. Christmas dinner.

She took a deep breath and looked around. Mrs. Courtney would go into hysterics if she saw her kitchen, but dinner was ready, only two hours later than she'd promised. The roasted turkey looked gorgeous. The scrape of chair legs on the floor of the dining room alerted her that Hank and Justin had arrived.

"What the hell?"

The shout from Justin sent her flying to the dining room. "What's the matter?"

Justin brushed past her, heading into the kitchen. "Spider mites," he said.

"Spider mites?" She watched in confusion as Hank tied the four corners of the tablecloth together, wrapping the fancy porcelain, elaborate silver and a centerpiece of evergreen boughs in a linen package. "What are you doing?"

Back from the kitchen, Justin carefully took the bundle from the table and carried it out the front door. Placing it on the ground, he opened one corner of the bundle and doused the contents with bug spray.

Cait, who'd raced after him, shrieked with horror. "What are you doing?"

"I told you, spider mites. The eggs must have been in the branches, and the heat in the house caused them to hatch. Their web covered the whole table. Don't worry, nothing broke."

"But my table." She'd been so proud of the elegant and artistic setting.

Justin gave her a commiserating smile as he guided her back into the house. "Don't worry. The food will taste as good on our regular dishes."

Cait walked into the kitchen and let out a blood-curdling scream. Hearing Justin guffawing behind her, she said furiously, "It's not funny." Her scream failed to disturb Lucy. The kitten had managed to get most of her body inside the huge turkey, only her rear end and striped tail giving away her presence. Snatching the opportunistic diner, Cait explored Lucy's mouth with a finger. "It would serve you right if you did choke on a bone. I am really, really angry with you." Wiping Lucy off with a paper towel, she set her on the floor.

Having washed his hands, Justin inspected the turkey. "If I carve off this large section of breast and remove the skin, we should be okay. Harry can wash the rest of the meat and boil it up for soup or something." Justin looked around. "It's not a tragedy. You've fixed enough food for an army."

"All right." She wouldn't let a little glitch in her plans upset her. Ranch wives coped. Justin put more plates and flatware on the table, and she carried in the food. Fortunately, she'd already removed the stuffing from the turkey before Lucy decided to turn taste tester.

"Looks and smells delicious," Hank said in a hearty voice.

"I'm sorry about the rolls. I forgot to set the timer."

"Nothing worse than rolls that aren't done." Justin set a blackened one on his plate.

"You don't have to eat it," Cait said. Somehow they looked more burned on the serving plate than they had in the kitchen on the baking sheet. "Try the stuffing," she urged the men.

Justin took a bite, got a funny look on his face and reached for water. After a long drink, he said, "Interesting. But good."

Cait immediately took a large bite. And gagged. "It's awful. I thought three cloves of garlic sounded excessive, but that's what the recipe said."

Hank picked at his stuffing with a fork, then held up a white chunk. "You put three of these in?"

"No. I put in three cloves. That's what the recipe said."

Hank and Justin looked at each other. Finally, Justin said carefully, "A garlic bulb is made up of a number of cloves."

Cait felt miserably stupid. "I put in the whole round thing. Three of them."

The two men doggedly tried everything on the table. The mashed potatoes had lumps the size of marbles, but it didn't matter because they'd scorched on the bottom and the burned taste tainted the entire batch. Too much salt had rendered the lumpy gravy inedible. The broccoli was overcooked and waterlogged; the hollandaise sauce had curdled, and the turkey was bone-dry and tasteless. Hank found a dead bug in his green salad.

Near tears, Cait put down her fork and shoved away her plate. "This is awful. It's all awful." Unable to meet Justin's gaze across the table, she looked past his shoulder. The mirror over the buffet behind him reflected her image back to her. Her own mother wouldn't recognize her. Her hair was a mess, flour decorated one side of her face, and chocolate was smeared on the other side. The entire menu could be read off her dress. "I'm sorry." She fought back tears. "The worst part is, all this food and you haven't had anything to eat."

"I'll fry up some hamburgers." Justin squeezed her shoulder as he headed for the kitchen. "Don't worry about it. You were a little overambitious. It could happen to anyone."

"Not Marilee," Cait said bitterly.

"If Marilee were here, we'd probably have tapioca pudding," Hank said.

Cait managed a smile. Just as she managed to eat the hamburger Justin fixed. The perfect hamburger. She'd never in her life fixed a hamburger that didn't turn out either still raw or burned to a crisp.

At least she had the pie. "Who's ready for dessert?" she asked brightly. "I made chocolate pie."

Hank quickly patted his stomach. "I'm stuffed. That was one really big hamburger."

Cait turned to Justin. He gave her a weak smile. "Sure. Sounds great."

She was in the kitchen when she heard Justin's low-pitched comment to his uncle. "Coward."

"Hell, Justin. I'm not young like you. I don't have a cast-iron stomach anymore."

"Maybe it'll be edible."

"Yeah, sure." Hank's chair scraped back. "You can have my piece."

Cait opened the refrigerator. In less than fifteen minutes, Hank was going to be begging for a piece of this pie. She'd make him sweat before she cut him a piece. The pie cradled in her hands, she swung around, bumping the refrigerator door shut with her hip, and headed toward the dining room.

Nick, taking advantage of a patch of linoleum warmed by the oven, lay sprawled in the middle of the floor. Cait had stepped over him seemingly a million times in the course of serving dinner. Now intent on the precious cargo in her hands, she forgot about him until her toe connected solidly with his hip. Nick let out a yelp and jumped up. Cait sprang backward, hanging grimly on to the pie plate. The sudden, jolting movement sent the filling, in one beautifully molded whole, sliding from the crust and sailing through the air, to land on the floor with a solid plop. Stunned, Cait stared at the metal pie plate that now held nothing more than a crust smeared with chocolate. "Damn, damn, damn!" Cait hurled the plate and crust across the kitchen.

The noise brought Justin. After one look, he exited as fast as he'd entered. Muted laughter came from the dining room.

Cait pushed Nick away from the chocolate filling. "Dogs shouldn't eat chocolate. How could you do this to me?"

"I'll clean it up."

"Go away." She took the paper towels Justin handed her and wiped up the mess. Justin, wisely, said nothing. Tossing the last filthy paper towel in the trash, Cait said, "I'll get a motel in town tonight and pack up my things tomorrow. I'm sure you can get your money back on the lens and stuff."

Justin pulled her to her feet and lifted her chin to wipe her face with a damp kitchen towel. "It's only a pie."

His kindness made things worse. She knew she could stay. She wanted to stay. Justin's home, his ranch, his horses, his body, all could be hers. He'd be kind and generous. Except he couldn't give her the one thing she wanted. His love.

Turning from him, she hunched over the sink. Justin didn't want her love, and without love, anything else she had to offer him meant nothing. She had only one thing worth giving to Justin. His freedom. He'd never ask her for it, and he'd be reluctant to take it, but she'd insist. She loved him too much to force him into living a loveless life.

"It's not just a pie," she said bleakly. "It's me. I can't do anything right. I never fitted in with my family, and I don't fit in here. I should never have married you. Any ignoramus could see you didn't want to marry me. No," she said, warding off his polite protest, "you admitted the other day you wouldn't have married me if you hadn't slept with me. Don't lie to me now. I forced you into marrying me and I acted like a spoiled brat the first year of our marriage. I don't blame you for anything."

"So you're going to hit and run again."

"Call it what you want. I came back because I thought, I hoped, this time things would be different." It was impossible for her to emulate his cool, emotionless voice. Wrenching on the faucet, she bathed her burning cheeks with cold water. "I thought in two years

I'd grown up, that I'd learned to be the kind of wife you wanted. I thought if I proved to you I could fit in, could belong on the ranch, then you'd fall..."

She swallowed. Her words were beginning to sound like a pathetic plea to be allowed to stay. Sympathy wasn't what she wanted from Justin. She tried again.

"I thought things would work out between us, but I was wrong, so I'm leaving. I know you won't stop me. You told me the choice was up to me." She turned blindly toward the door.

"You forgot to mention you love me."

If she said she did, he'd convince her to stay. "I don't love you." She managed to get her feet moving again.

"Nick."

The low command came from behind her as a sharp bark brought her up short. Blinking tears from her eyes, she saw Nick blocking the doorway. "Get out of my way, Nick." The dog barked again, sharp warning barks. Cait took a tentative step. Nick erupted in a frenzy of barking. Cait froze. "Justin, what's wrong with Nick?"

"He's just doing his job."

Cait pivoted slowly. Justin's shoulders were propped against the refrigerator, his arms folded across his chest. The merest hint of a smile curved his lips. His eyes laughed at her. She wanted to slug him. She wanted to throw herself in his arms. She contented herself with asking in a controlled voice, "Would you please explain that?"

"His job is herding cows. I told him to bring in a stray."

A variety of emotions assaulted her. She clung to anger. "That's not funny. Call him off. You promised I could choose whether I wanted to stay or leave. I want to leave."

"I guess I didn't make myself clear. If you couldn't stand ranch living or couldn't stand me, hell, I'd help you pack. But seeing as how you like living on the ranch and love me..." Justin straightened up and moved toward her.

"I don't love you." A low growl halted Cait's backward retreat. "Justin, please."

He put a hand over her mouth. "No begging, Cait." He gripped the back of her head with his other hand. "Begging isn't for the likes of you and me. We work for what we want." He must have felt her lips move, because he grinned and said, "Don't bite me. I've got something to say and I'm going to say it. If I move my hand, you'll start jabbering, and if you bite me, we'll end up on the kitchen floor. We don't want to embarrass Nick."

Cait sputtered against his palm, but she kept her teeth to herself. The heated look in his eyes backed up his threat. She locked her hands behind her to prevent her traitorous arms from wrapping themselves around his warmth.

"First, we'll dispense with this nonsense that you don't love me. Don't shake your head. If I ever had any doubts, you put them to rest the day you dumped me from the pickup. The way you came barreling through those cows, shoving them out of your way as if they were cardboard cutouts was pretty damned convincing, considering it's no secret you're terrified of cows."

He couldn't possibly have understood her muffled words, so he must be a mind reader.

"Hell, there was nothing in our marriage vows that said you had to like cows. When I walked into your New York apartment and saw you, how you felt about cows was the last thing on my mind." His mouth quirked as she went very still. "Getting interested in my conversation, are you?"

He laughed at her negative head shake. "You'll have to bear with me anyway. You reminded me of a young filly, full of promise. Those long legs, black hair, blue eyes—damn, I wished you were a couple years older and anybody but a rich city girl. Then I discovered you were funny and lively and smart and interested in everything that went on. You asked the doorman about his ill daughter, discussed world affairs with the man at the newsstand and enjoyed looking at the photos of grandchildren belonging to the lady in the little flower shop around the corner. I realized beneath the smart exterior lived a person who cared about others, but even realizing you knew by name every dog and cat in a ten-mile radius didn't blind me to the knowledge that ranch life wasn't for a girl like you."

His eyes darkened. "Then we went horseback riding, and suddenly the impossible started seeming possible. I thought maybe I'd keep in touch and in two or three years I'd go back to New York and, well, see how things went."

A hoarseness crept into his voice. "I'm sorry I lost control and rushed you into marriage. So yes, if I had to do it all over again, I'd do it differently. You were young and spoiled, and Hank and the others, they were so sure you'd hate it here, they were too critical. I could have been a lot more patient and understanding. And talked to you more. I wasn't used to having a woman around. I didn't know what you needed."

He cleared his throat. "And I didn't want to care. I thought you'd fallen in love with the myth of marrying a cowboy and living on a ranch, and then when you came out here, you hated the reality. I knew, deep inside, you were going to leave me, and I wanted you to do it before it was too late. Before I couldn't let you go. When you finally left, I assumed you'd go home, get a divorce, and after a while the year would be nothing but a minor blip in your life.''

Cait gabbled against his palm.

He tipped back her head. "I missed you so damned much. Kidded myself I'd look up and see you riding over a hill. Wanted your bottom tucked up against me at night.'' His fingers tightened in her hair. "I hated the sight of Pikes Peak reminding me you were on the other side, knowing in a couple of hours I could be in the Springs and haul you back. But I loved you too much to force you to return.''

Cait kicked him in the shin, shocking him into releasing her. "You are the stupidest man on this earth. For two years I've been working and agonizing and planning and hoping and fearing... If you'd ever once—'' she looked wildly around the kitchen, searching for something to throw at him, something to dent his stupid head so maybe a little common sense could filter its way in ''—just once mentioned the word *love*—''

"I tried to show you—''

"Show me!'' she shrieked. "What kind of idiot are you?'' Her gaze landed on the whipped cream she'd prepared to go with the pie. With a quick sweep of her hand, she grabbed a glob of cream and threw it in Justin's face. Instantly she knew she'd made a major mistake.

Picking up the bowl, Justin stalked her across the kitchen, quickly cornering her. He scooped up a handful of whipped cream, his gaze never leaving her. Cait squeezed her eyes closed. Justin laughed softly and then, pressing her tightly into the corner with his hips, he ripped open her blouse. Buttons flew helter-skelter across the room. Cait opened her mouth to protest and received a mouthful of sweet cream. Before she could swallow it, Justin slipped off her bra and frosted her chest. Her nipples immediately contracted from the cold. Justin began methodically licking off the cream. She had to cling to something or collapse. Justin's neck was the only something around.

"Tell me, Cait—" Justin's voice was muffled against her skin "—that you don't love me."

"You don't play fair."

"I'm not playing." His mouth traveled up to press a quick kiss against her lips before he pulled together her blouse and wrapped his arms around her, shielding her from the doorway.

"What the hell is going on out here?" Hank roared from across the room. "Can't a man take a nap on Christmas Day?"

"We're cleaning up the kitchen," Justin said with a laugh in his voice. "Go back to your nap."

Hours later, Cait lay awake. Her body reposed in a pleasant, sated condition, but she couldn't turn off her mind. Outside, a chorus of coyotes sent their yipping voices into the night sky.

"Christmas carols," said a lazy voice at her side.

She rolled over to rest her elbows on Justin's firm chest and shared her thoughts. "I was thinking maybe Mrs. Courtney would teach me how to cook, and really, I think I can get used to cows."

Justin's chest shook with subdued laughter. "Can they get used to you?"

"Justin, I'm serious. I want to be a good rancher's wife."

He heaved a deep sigh and, gently putting her from him, hauled his length out of bed. "C'mon. Get up."

"Get up? Now?" She looked at the clock. "It's two in the morning. Why are you getting up now?"

"Because." Justin whipped the covers from her bare body. "You've got three seconds or you're going the way you are."

"Going where?" Cait crawled out of bed and fumbled into her jeans and boots and a sweatshirt. "It's the middle of the night," she complained. "The stupid cows are probably asleep."

"This has nothing to do with cows." He jammed his hands into the back pockets of his jeans and glared at her. "I've had it with this perfect rancher's wife fixation you have. You yammered about it the entire time we were cleaning up the kitchen, and you'd still be harping on it in the shower if I hadn't changed the subject."

She could feel herself blush at the memory of exactly how and to what he'd changed the subject. "I don't see—"

"Then it's time you did," he said fiercely. "The hell with cooking lessons and cows. You only need two things to be the perfect rancher's wife. A rancher husband—you got that—and the right kind of transportation."

The crazy, unbelievable notion took hold of Cait that Justin was glaring and practically yelling at her because he was nervous. As if Rosie wouldn't be the perfect gift.

His face darkened. "Quit grinning like an idiot and get moving."

A dozen mountain lions couldn't have stopped her, and minutes later she was half running down the dirt road trying to keep up with Justin's long strides. "This isn't the way to the barn," she said in surprise.

"Who said anything about going to the barn?"

"You said transportation...I thought..." She shrugged in the dark. "A horse..."

"What's wrong with Rosie? I thought you liked her."

She ran into him as he stopped abruptly in the road. "I do like Rosie, but she's yours."

"Why the hell would I buy Rosie back if not for you?"

"I thought, well, for breeding."

"You can breed her if you want." He resumed his rapid pace. After a minute he said, "I thought you knew she was your horse. I guess I should have said something."

"Justin." Cait grabbed his arm, forcing him to stop. "I love you."

"Good." He pulled her along with him.

Overhead, the stars seemed close enough to pluck from the sky. "At least tell me where we're going," Cait said.

"Court and Harry's place."

"Are you crazy? At this time of night."

"They're not there."

In front of the garage, Justin tied a cotton bandanna over her eyes. "Don't peek."

She heard him walk off, heard the scrabble of a key in the lock of the side door, and then a minute later, the large automatic door rumbled open.

Justin's hands were warm on her shoulders as he guided her forward a couple of steps. "I planned to give you this on the twenty-seventh. The other thing you need besides me to be a rancher's wife." He removed the bandanna. "Happy Anniversary."

The large glossy pickup truck parked in the Courtneys' garage was bright red. Cait burst into tears.

"Hey," Justin said in alarm, "if you don't like it, I can take it back."

Cait shook her head and flung her arms around Justin's middle. His arms enfolded her tightly. "It's the most wonderful gift anyone has ever given me," she blubbered into his coat, "but I don't have an anniversary present for you."

"The only thing I ever wanted is a wife who's perfect for me." Justin tipped up Cait's tear-drenched face. "And I have her."

INSTANT WIN 4229 SWEEPSTAKES
OFFICIAL RULES

1. NO PURCHASE NECESSARY. YOU ARE DEFINITELY A WINNER. For eligibility, play your instant win ticket and claim your prize as per instructions contained thereon. If your "Instant Win" ticket is missing or you wish another, send a self-addressed, stamped envelope (WA residents need not affix return postage) to: Instant Win 4229 Ticket, P.O. Box 9045, Buffalo, NY 14269-9045 in the U.S., and in Canada, P.O. Box 609, Fort Erie, Ontario, L2A 5X3. Only one (1) "Instant Win" ticket will be sent per outer mailing envelope. Requests received after 12/30/96 will not be honored.

2. Prize claims received after 1/15/97 will be deemed ineligible and will not be fulfilled. The exact prize value of each Instant Win ticket will be determined by comparing returned tickets with a prize value distribution list that has been preselected at random by computer. Prizes are valued in U.S. currency. For each one million, or part thereof, tickets distributed, the following prizes will be made available: 1 at $2,500 cash; 1 at $1,000 cash; 3 at $250 cash each; 5 at $50 cash each; 10 at $25 cash each; 1,000 at $1 cash each; and the balance at 50¢ cash each. Unclaimed prizes will not be awarded.

3. Winner claims are subject to verification by D. L. Blair, Inc., an independent judging organization whose decisions on all matters relating to this sweepstakes are final. Any returned tickets that are mutilated, tampered with, illegible or contain printing or other errors will be deemed automatically void. No responsibility is assumed for lost, late, nondelivered or misdirected mail. Taxes are the sole responsibility of winners. Limit: One (1) prize to a family, household or organization.

4. Offer open only to residents of the U.S. and Canada, 18 years of age or older, except employees of Harlequin Enterprises Limited, D. L. Blair, Inc., their agents and members of their immediate families. All federal, state, provincial, municipal and local laws apply. Offer void in Puerto Rico, the province of Quebec and wherever prohibited by law. All winners will receive their prize by mail. Taxes and/or duties are the sole responsibility of the winners. No substitution for prizes permitted. Major prize winners may be asked to sign and return an Affidavit of Eligibility within 30 days of notification. Noncompliance within this time or return of affidavit as undeliverable may result in disqualification, and prize may never be awarded. By acceptance of a prize, winners consent to the use of their names, photographs or other likeness for purposes of advertising, trade and promotion on behalf of Harlequin Enterprises Limited, without further compensation, unless prohibited by law. In order to win a prize, residents of Canada will be required to correctly answer a time-limited arithmetical skill-testing question to be administered by mail.

5. For a list of major prize winners (available after 2/14/97), send a self-addressed, stamped envelope to: "Instant Win 4229 Sweepstakes" Major Prize Winners, P.O. Box 4200, Blair, NE 68009-4200, U.S.A.

MILLION DOLLAR SWEEPSTAKES
OFFICIAL RULES
NO PURCHASE NECESSARY TO ENTER

1. To enter, follow the directions published. Method of entry may vary. For eligibility, entries must be received no later than March 31, 1998. No liability is assumed for printing errors, lost, late, non-delivered or misdirected entries.
   To determine winners, the sweepstakes numbers assigned to submitted entries will be compared against a list of randomly, preselected prize winning numbers. In the event all prizes are not claimed via the return of prize winning numbers, random drawings will be held from among all other entries received to award unclaimed prizes.

2. Prize winners will be determined no later than June 30, 1998. Selection of winning numbers and random drawings are under the supervision of D. L. Blair, Inc., an independent judging organization whose decisions are final. Limit: one prize to a family or organization. No substitution will be made for any prize, except as offered. Taxes and duties on all prizes are the sole responsibility of winners. Winners will be notified by mail. Odds of winning are determined by the number of eligible entries distributed and received.

3. Sweepstakes open to residents of the U.S. (except Puerto Rico), Canada and Europe who are 18 years of age or older, except employees and immediate family members of Torstar Corp., D. L. Blair, Inc., their affiliates, subsidiaries and all other agencies, entities, and persons connected with the use, marketing or conduct of this sweepstakes. All applicable laws and regulations apply. Sweepstakes offer void wherever prohibited by law. Any litigation within the province of Quebec respecting the conduct and awarding of a prize in this sweepstakes must be submitted to the Régie des alcools, des courses et des jeux. In order to win a prize, residents of Canada will be required to correctly answer a time-limited arithmetical skill-testing question to be administered by mail.

4. Winners of major prizes (Grand through Fourth) will be obligated to sign and return an Affidavit of Eligibility and Release of Liability within 30 days of notification. In the event of non-compliance within this time period or if a prize is returned as undeliverable, D. L. Blair, Inc. may at its sole discretion, award that prize to an alternate winner. By acceptance of their prize, winners consent to use of their names, photographs or other likeness for purposes of advertising, trade and promotion on behalf of Torstar Corp., its affiliates and subsidiaries, without further compensation unless prohibited by law. Torstar Corp. and D. L. Blair, Inc., their affiliates and subsidiaries are not responsible for errors in printing of sweepstakes and prize winning numbers. In the event a duplication of a prize winning number occurs, a random drawing will be held from among all entries received with that prize winning number to award that prize.

5. This sweepstakes is presented by Torstar Corp., its subsidiaries and affiliates in conjunction with book, merchandise and/or product offerings. The number of prizes to be awarded and their value are as follows: Grand Prize — $1,000,000 (payable at $33,333.33 a year for 30 years); First Prize — $50,000; Second Prize — $10,000; Third Prize — $5,000; 3 Fourth Prizes — $1,000 each; 10 Fifth Prizes — $250 each; 1,000 Sixth Prizes — $10 each. Values of all prizes are in U.S. currency. Prizes in each level will be presented in different creative executions, including various currencies, vehicles, merchandise and travel. Any presentation of a prize level in a currency other than U.S. currency represents an approximate equivalent to the U.S. currency prize for that level, at that time. Prize winners will have the opportunity of selecting any prize offered for that level; however, the actual non U.S. currency equivalent prize if offered and selected, shall be awarded at the exchange rate existing at 3:00 P.M. New York time on March 31, 1998. A travel prize option, if offered and selected by winner, must be completed within 12 months of selection and is subject to: traveling companion(s) completing and returning of a Release of Liability prior to travel; and hotel and flight accommodations availability. For a current list of all prize options offered within prize levels, send a self-addressed, stamped envelope (WA residents need not affix postage) to: MILLION DOLLAR SWEEPSTAKES Prize Options, P.O. Box 4456, Blair, NE 68009-4456, USA.

6. For a list of prize winners (available after July 31, 1998) send a separate, stamped, self-addressed envelope to: MILLION DOLLAR SWEEPSTAKES Winners, P.O. Box 4459, Blair, NE 68009-4459, USA.

EXTRA BONUS PRIZE DRAWING
NO PURCHASE OR OBLIGATION NECESSARY TO ENTER

7. The Extra Bonus Prize will be awarded in a random drawing to be conducted no later than 5/30/98 from among all entries received. To qualify, entries must be received by 3/31/98 and comply with published directions. Prize ($50,000) is valued in U.S. currency. Prize will be presented in different creative expressions, including various currencies, vehicles, merchandise and travel. Any presentation in a currency other than U.S. currency represents an approximate equivalent to the U.S. currency value at that time. Prize winner will have the opportunity of selecting any prize offered in any presentation of the Extra Bonus Prize Drawing; however, the actual non U.S. currency equivalent prize, if offered and selected by winner, shall be awarded at the exchange rate existing at 3:00 P.M. New York time on March 31, 1998. For a current list of prize options offered, send a self-addressed, stamped envelope (WA residents need not affix postage) to: Extra Bonus Prize Options, P.O. Box 4462, Blair, NE 68009-4462, USA. All eligibility requirements and restrictions of the MILLION DOLLAR SWEEPSTAKES apply. Odds of winning are dependent upon number of eligible entries received. No substitution for prize except as offered. For the name of winner (available after 7/31/98), send a self-addressed, stamped envelope to: Extra Bonus Prize Winner, P.O. Box 4463, Blair, NE 68009-4463, USA.

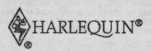